A RUN-IN ON THE MOORS

Doctor Who ran from the landrover as fast as he could, undeterred by the gathering darkness and the uneven ground. His long legs took him across the moor at a tremendous speed, tartan scarf flying out behind him. But fast as the Doctor was, the Loch Ness monster was even faster. The next roar was so loud that he felt it must be breathing down his neck.

The Zygon meanwhile was preparing to enjoy the death of the Doctor from a front row seat. A special monitor screen, linked to the optical system of the Loch Ness monster, showed him the scene on the moor through the monster's eyes.

The Doctor was tiring fast now. Already he seemed to have covered most of Tulloch Moor. He dodged and weaved, used every scrap of cover, but the huge creature behind him matched his every move.

Finally, inevitably, the Doctor slipped. His foot turned in a patch of mud, and he crashed to the ground, half-stunned. It took him a moment to recover his breath, and as he started to scramble to his feet, he saw it was too late. The monster was almost upon him.

The Zygon felt as if he were the Loch Ness monster, looking down from his mighty height at the puny figure of the Doctor. "Kill him," hissed the Zygon, "kill him!"

Through the cold, misty darkness of the moor, the Doctor saw the savage head of the monster lunge toward him. . . .

(please turn page)

THE FOURTH DOCTOR WHO

This episode features the fourth Doctor Who, who has survived three reincarnations. The long trailing scarf, the floppy wide-brimmed hat, the mop of curly hair and the wide-eyed stare—all these are the obvious trademarks of the fourth Doctor Who. Along with a delightful mix of personality traits: genius and clown, hero and buffoon —the fourth Doctor Who combines the best of all who preceded him.

DOCTOR WHO'S COMPANIONS

SARAH JANE SMITH

Sarah is an independent freelance journalist. She has a mind of her own and once, while in search of a story, stowed away on Doctor Who's TARDIS—and ended up in the medieval past. Forever swearing she will never again set foot in the TARDIS, Sarah cannot resist the Doctor's plea that she accompany him one more time. While Sarah appears quite invulnerable, she really does need a bit of protection now and then.

THE BRIGADIER

Brigadier Alastair Lethbridge-Stewart is the Commanding Officer of the British branch of UNIT. UNIT, by the way, is the United Nations Intelligence Taskforce, created to protect the Planet Earth from extraterrestrial invasion. The Brigadier is everyone's idea of the typical British officer—his voice is clipped, his manner is abrupt, and his mustache is neat. But he is hardly robot-like. In fact, he's quite bright and his several encounters with alien species and his long and stormy association with the Doctor have made him very flexible. He's really very fond of the eccentric Doctor but sometimes he finds him very difficult to work with.

DOCTOR WHO

AND THE LOCH NESS MONSTER
Terrance Dicks

with an Introduction by
Harlan Ellison

PINNACLE BOOKS • NEW YORK

DOCTOR WHO AND THE
LOCH NESS MONSTER (#6)

Copyright © 1976 by Terrance Dicks and Robert Banks Stewart
"Doctor Who" series copyright © 1975 by British Broadcasting Corporation.
Introduction copyright © 1979 by Harlan Ellison

A Pinnacle Books edition, published by special arrangement with W.H. Allen & Co., Ltd. First published in Great Britain by Universal-Tandem Publishing Co., Ltd. 1976

First printing, June 1979
Second printing, June 1979
Third printing, November 1981

ISBN: 0-523-41791-8

Cover illustration by David Mann

Printed in the United States of America

PINNACLE BOOKS, INC.
1430 Broadway
New York, New York 10018

Contents

Introducing *DOCTOR WHO*

amenities performed by
HARLAN ELLISON

They could not have been more offended, confused, enraged and startled. . . . There was a moment of stunned silence . . . and then an eruption of angry voices from all over the fifteen-hundred-person audience. The kids in their Luke Skywalker pajamas (cobbled up from older brother's castoff karate *gi*) and the retarded adults spot-welded into their Darth Vader fright-masks howled with fury. But I stood my ground, there on the lecture platform at the World Science Fiction Convention, and I repeated the heretical words that had sent them into animal hysterics:

"*Star Wars* is adolescent nonsense; *Close Encounters* is obscurantist drivel; 'Star Trek' can turn your brains to purée of bat guano; and the greatest science fiction series of all time is *Doctor Who*! And I'll take you all on, one-by-one or all in a bunch to back it up!"

Auditorium monitors moved in, truncheons ready to club down anyone foolish enough to try jumping the lecture platform; and finally there was relative silence. And I heard scattered voices screaming from the back of the room, "Who?" And I said, "Yes. Who!"

(It was like that old Abbott and Costello routine: Who's on first? No, Who's on third; What's on first.)

After a while we got it all sorted out and they understood that when I said Who I didn't mean *whom*, I meant Who . . . Doctor Who . . . the most famous science fiction character on British television. The renegade Time Lord, the far traveler through Time and Space, the sword of justice from the planet Gallifrey, the scourge of villains and monsters the galaxy over. The one and only, the incomparable, the bemusing and bewildering Doctor Who, the humanistic defender of Good and Truth whose exploits put to shame those of Kimball Kinnison, Captain Future and pantywaist-nerds like Han Solo and Luke Skywalker.

My hero! Doctor Who!

For the American reading (and television-viewing) audience (and in this sole, isolated case I hope they're one and the same) *Doctor Who* is a new factor in the equation of fantastic literature. Since 1963 the Doctor and his exploits have been a consistent element of British culture. But we're only now being treated to the wonderful universes of Who here in the States. For those of us who were exposed to both the TV series on BBC and the long series of *Doctor Who* novels published in Great Britain, the time of solitary proselytizing is at an end. All we need to do now is thrust a Who novel into the hands of the unknowledgeable, or drag the unwary to a TV set and turn it on as the good Doctor goes through his paces. That's all it takes. Try this book and you'll understand.

I envy you your first exposure to this amazing conceit. And I wish for you the same delight I felt when Michael Moorcock, the finest fantasist in the English-speaking world, sat me down in front of his set in London, turned on the telly, and said, "Now be quiet and just watch."

That was in 1975. And I've been hooked on "Doctor Who" ever since. Understand: I despise television (having written it for sixteen years) and I spend much of my time urging people to bash in their picture tubes with Louisville Sluggers, to free themselves of the monster of the coaxial cable. And so, you must perceive that I speak of something utterly extraordinary and marvelous when I suggest you watch the "Doctor Who" series in whatever syndicated slot your local station has scheduled it. You must recognize that I risk all credibility for future exhortations by telling you *this* TV viewing will not harm you . . . will, in fact, delight and uplift you, stretch your imagination, tickle your risibilities, flense your intellect of all lesser visual sf affections, improve your disposition and clean up your zits. What I'm saying here, case you're a *yotz* who needs things codified simply and directly, is that "Doctor Who" is the apex, the pinnacle, the tops, the Louvre Museum, the tops, the Coliseum, and other etcetera.

Now to give you a few basic facts about the Doctor, to brighten your path through this nifty series of lunatic novels.

He is a Time Lord: one of that immensely wise and powerful super-race of alien beings who, for centuries unnumbered, have watched and studied all of Time and Space with intellects (as H.G. Wells put it) vast and cool and unsympathetic. Their philosophy was never to interfere in the affairs of alien races, merely to watch and wait.

But one of their number, known only as the Doctor, found such inaction anathema. As he studied the interplay of great forces in the cosmos, the endless wars and invasions, the entropic conflict between Good and Evil, the rights and lives of a thousand alien life-forms debased and brutalized, the wrongs left unrighted . . . he was overcome by the compulsion *to act*! He was a renegade, a misfit in the name of justice.

And so he stole a TARDIS and fled.

Ah, yes. The TARDIS. That most marvelous device for spanning the Time-lines and traversing all of known/unknown Space. The name is an acronym for Time And Relative Dimensions In Space. Marvelous! An amazing machine that can change shape to fit in with any locale in which it materializes. But the TARDIS stolen from his fellow Time Lords by the Doctor was in for repairs. And so it was frozen in the shape of its first appearance: a British police call box. Those of you who have been to England may have seen such call boxes. (There are very few of them extant currently, because the London "bobbies" now have two-way radio in their patrol cars; but before the advent of that communication system the tall, dark blue street call box—something like our old-fashioned wooden phone booth—was a familiar sight in the streets of London. If a police officer needed assistance he could call in directly from such a box, and if the station house wanted to get in touch with a copper they could turn on the big blue light atop the box and its flashing would attract a "bobby.")

Further wonder: the outward size of the TARDIS does not reveal its relative size *inside*. The size of a phone booth outwardly, it is enormous within, holding many sections filled with the Doctor's super-scientific equipment.

Unfortunately, the stolen TARDIS needed more repairs than just the fixing of its shape-changing capabilities. Its steering mechanism was also wonky, and so the Doctor could never be certain that the coordinates he set for time and place of materializing would be correct. He might set course for the planet Karn . . . and wind up in Victorian London. He might wish to relax at an intergalactic pleasure resort . . . and pop into existence in Antarctica. He might lay in a course for the deadly gold mines of Voga . . . and appear in Renaissance Italy.

It makes for a chancy existence, but the Doctor takes it all unflinchingly. As do his attractive female traveling companions, whose liaisons with the Doctor are never sufficiently explicated for those of us with a nasty, suspicious turn of mind.

The Doctor *looks* human and, apart from his quirky way of thinking, even *acts* human most of the time. But he is a Time Lord, not a mere mortal. He has two hearts, a stable body temperature of 60°, and—not to stun you too much—he's approximately 750 years old. Or at least he was that age when the first of the 43 *Doctor Who* novels was written. God (or Time Lords) only knows how old he is now!

Only slightly less popular than the good Doctor himself are his arch-foes and the distressing alien monsters he battles through the pages of these wild books and in phosphor-dot reality on your TV screens. They seem endless in their variety: the Vardans, the Oracle, Fendahl, the virus swarm of the Purpose, The Master, the Tong of the Black Scorpion, the evil brain of Morbius, the mysterious energy force known as the Mandragora Helix, the android clone Kraals, the Zygons, the Cybermen, the Ice Warriors, the Autons, the spore beast called the Krynoid and—most deadly and menacing of them all—the robot threat of the Daleks.

Created by mad Davros, the great Kaled scientist, the pepper-pot-shaped Daleks made such an impression in England when they were first introduced into the series that they became a cultural artifact almost immediately. Movies have been made about them, toys have been manufactured of Daleks, coloring books, Dalek candies, soaps, slippers, Easter eggs and even special Dalek fireworks. They rival the Doctor for the attention of a fascinated audience and they have been brought back again and again during the fourteen years the series has perpetuated itself on BBC television; and their shiveringly pleasurable manifestations have not been confined just to England and America. Doctor Who and the Daleks have millions of rabid fans in over thirty countries around the world.

Like the three fictional characters *every* nation knows—Sherlock Holmes, Tarzan and Superman—Doctor Who seems to have a universal appeal.

Let me conclude this paean of praise with these thoughts: hating *Star Wars* and "Star Trek" is not a difficult chore for me. I recoil from that sophomoric species of creation that excuses its simplistic cliche structure and homage to the transitory (as does *Star Wars*) as violently as I do from that which sententiously purports to be deep and intellectual when it is, in fact, superficial self-conscious twaddle (as does "Star Trek"). This is not to say that I am an ivory tower intellect whose doubledome can only support Proust or Descartes. When I was a little kid, and was reading everything I could lay hands on, I read the classics with joy, but enjoyed equally those works I've come to think of as "elegant trash": the Edgar Rice Burroughs novels, The Shadow, Doc Savage, Conan, comic books and Uncle Wiggly. They taught me a great deal of what I know about courage and truth and ethic in the world.

To that list I add *Doctor Who*. His adventures are sunk to the hips in humanism, decency, solid adventure and simple good reading. They are not classics, make no mistake. They can never touch the illuminative level of Dickens or Mark Twain or Kafka. But they are solid entertainment based on an understanding of Good and Evil in the world. They say to us, "You, too, can be Doctor Who. You, like the good Doctor, can stand up for that which is bright and bold and true. You can shape the world, if you'll only go and try."

And they do it in the form of *all* great literature . . . the cracking good, well-plotted adventure yarn. They are direct lineal heirs to the adventures of Rider Haggard and Talbot Mundy, of H.G. Wells and Jules Verne, of Mary Shelley and Ray Bradbury. They are worth your time.

And if you give yourself up to the Doctor's winsome ways, he will take substance and reality in your imagination. For that reason, for the inestimable goodness and delight in every *Doctor Who* adventure, for the benefits he proffers, I lend my name and my urging to read and watch him.

I don't think you'll do less than thank me for shoving you down with this book in your hands, and telling you . . . here's Who. Meet the Doctor.

The pleasure is all mine. And all yours, kiddo.

HARLAN ELLISON
Los Angeles

DOCTOR WHO
AND THE LOCH NESS MONSTER

1

Death from the Sea

The oil rig called "Bonnie Prince Charlie" towered high above the moonlit sea. Its massive steel legs, set firm in their concrete foundations, seemed to defy the ocean, which lapped almost tamely around the base of the rig. It was a calm, clear night, silent except for the persistent sighing of a chill wind.

In the warmth and comfort of the rig's radio room Jock Munro stretched out in his chair, a mug of rum-laced cocoa in one hand, his radio mike in the other. He was ordering fresh provisions from the supply base on the Scottish mainland, more for the sake of a chat than because the matter was urgent. "Hey, and listen, Willie, the blokes say can you rustle up a few haggis and send 'em out with tomorrow's supply helicopter? The cook here's a Sassenach, and he doesna' ken the first thing about them!"

Grinning to himself, he waited for Willie to demand how the blanketty-blank he was supposed to find haggis for twenty-odd men at a few hours' notice.

But Willie's reply did not come. The radio

went suddenly dead. Jock jiggled controls for a bit, cursed, and tried again. "This is Charlie Rig to Hibernian Control—are you receiving? I say again, Charlie Rig to Hibernian Control, do you read me?" The only reply was a high-pitched electronic burbling sound.

Suddenly the entire rig shuddered under a tremendous jolt. Munro was thrown out of his chair and sent crashing against the door. As he struggled to his feet, there came a second jolt, and then another. The rig seemed to reel under a series of massive hammer blows. Munro struggled to the RT set. "Mayday, Mayday, Hibernian Control and all shipping . . . the rig is breaking up . . ."

Another tremendous blow tilted the entire cabin, sending the RT set crashing to the floor. Munro struggled to the door and clambered out onto the catwalk. From all around he could hear the blaring of alarm signals, the shouts and screams of running men. Clinging to a steel girder, he gazed out at the moonlit sea. To his horror, he saw something huge, incredible, rushing through the water toward the rig. As it struck again, the impact sent the whole rig lurching. Munro was torn loose from his girder and sent flying through the air. He struck the water with an impact that knocked the breath from him, and the cold, dark sea closed over his head.

* * *

With a strange, wheezing, groaning sound, the blue police call box materialized on the bleak windswept hillside. The door opened and three people emerged. First came a very tall man, untidily dressed in a strange assortment of vaguely bohemian-looking garments. A long woolly scarf dangled around his neck and a floppy hat was jammed on the back of a tangle of curly hair. He looked around eagerly, his eyes ablaze with interest. A broad, child-like grin spread over his face at the sight of the wild and unfriendly landscape.

The two who followed from the call box didn't look quite so delighted. The first was a brawny young man, conventionally dressed in blazer and flannels. His handsome face with its square jaw, frank blue eyes, and curly hair, made him look like the hero of an old-fashioned adventure story. The slim, attractive girl who accompanied him shivered in the cold wind, turning up the collar of her jacket.

The young man was Harry Sullivan, the girl Sarah Jane Smith. Both stared accusingly at their companion, that mysterious traveler in Time and Space known only as the Doctor.

Sarah looked startled, "I thought you said we were returning to Earth."

The Doctor abandoned his survey of the landscape to give her a look of guileless innocence. "This *is* Earth, Sarah."

"If you say so, Doctor." She didn't sound too convinced. Suddenly the blue police call box winked out of existence. Sarah clutched the Doctor's arm. "The TARDIS—it's gone."

The Doctor sighed. The TARDIS—the initials stood for Time and Relative Dimensions in Space—was playing up more and more these days. As fast as he repaired one thing, something else went wrong. "Thought I'd fixed that fusion plate," he muttered crossly. "Must have gone on the blink again. Shan't be two seconds." He stepped inside the invisible TARDIS and immediately became invisible himself.

Sarah and Harry watched unsurprised. Since beginning their travels through Time and Space with the Doctor they'd seen so many strange things that the odd vanishing trick was nothing special.

Sarah looked again at the windswept landscape. "I don't care what he says, this isn't Earth."

Harry said gloomily, "Probably some benighted planet right on the far edge of the galaxy." Sarah and Harry knew from experience that the TARDIS's destinations were always unpredictable, though this never seemed to affect the Doctor's cheerful confidence.

The TARDIS reappeared and so did the Doctor. He was wearing a strange-looking bonnet with a bobble on top, and the woolly scarf had been replaced by another, equally long, in a particularly vivid tartan. "Native dress," he explained. "We don't want to attract attention now we're in Scotland."

"How do you know?" asked Harry suspiciously.

The Doctor breathed deeply of the clear cold air. "I can smell the tangle of the isles. Besides, I've just checked the co-ordinates. Now why has the Brigadier brought us here?"

Brigadier Alastair Lethbridge-Stewart was head of the British section of UNIT, the United Nations Intelligence Taskforce, an organization of which Harry Sullivan was a member. UNIT was dedicated to protecting Earth from the many attacks and invasions from outer space that had plagued it in recent years. The development of Man's technology to the point where the moon had already been reached, with interplanetary travel an inevitable next step, had attracted the attention of hostile forces throughout the galaxy. Most seemed to consider the Earth an attractive little planet, just ripe for conquest. UNIT had been formed to help Earth protect itself, and the Doctor was supposed to be UNIT's Scientific Adviser. Unfortunately, he hated being tied down to one place or time, and his habit of disappearing on prolonged trips around the galaxy was a constant source of aggravation to the Brigadier.

Just before this latest trip, the two had reached a compromise. The Doctor had given the Brigadier a recall device, which could signal to the TARDIS whenever and wherever it happened to be; he had also given his promise to return the Earth whenever the signal was used.

Watched by Harry and Sarah, the Doctor produced a compass-like device from his pocket. He flipped open the lid, revealing a directional needle quivering over a multi-colored dial. "Well, he's still signaling on the syonic scale. All we have to do is keep the needle in the green sector and it'll lead us to him. Follow me!"

Tartan scarf blowing in the wind, the Doctor set off down the hillside. Sarah and Harry followed. Despite all the Doctor's assurances they were quite prepared to come across anything from a Dalek to a dinosaur.

What they did meet was considerably more prosaic. The track joined up with a narrow country lane, and after consulting his syonic compass the Doctor led them along it. A few moments later they heard the sound of an engine, and a muddy station wagon appeared on the road behind them. As it came up to them, it stopped. The driver was an authoritative-looking old fellow in country tweeds. He spoke in a clipped, upper-class voice, with just a suggestion of a Highland lilt somewhere underneath. "Might I offer you a lift?"

The Doctor took a quick look at his compass. "Well, you do seem to be going our way. It's extremely kind of you."

"Whom do I have the pleasure of speaking to?"

"Forgive me. This is Sarah Jane Smith, this is Harry Sullivan, and I'm the Doctor."

The driver of the station wagon gave a stiff nod. "I am the Duke of Forgill. Would you like to get in?"

The Doctor climbed in beside the Duke, and Sarah and Harry piled in the back.

As they drove down the lane, the Doctor said, "I wonder if you could tell me where we are?"

"You're just outside the village of Tulloch."

"And Tulloch is . . . ?"

The Duke looked at him curiously. "In the highlands of Scotland, of course. As a matter of fact, we're quite close to Loch Ness."

Sarah noticed a lumpy tarpaulin-covered object in the area behind the back seat. From under the tarpaulin a glassy eye stared at her. She lifted the cloth a little, then smiled. The covered object was a stuffed stag's head, mounted on a wooden plaque.

Brigadier Lethbridge-Stewart was not a happy man. The landlord of Tulloch Village Inn had resented having his parlor commandeered by UNIT for their temporary HQ. He was retaliating by constant practice on the bagpipes. The noise had already given the Brigadier a headache. Now a very angry oil company executive called Huckle was pounding the table and shouting at him. The Doctor still hadn't appeared, though his signaling device was bleeping away in the corner. To crown it all, the Brigadier was beginning to have second thoughts about his decision to celebrate his return to the land of his ancestors by wearing the kilt. He had a shrewd suspicion that he looked ridiculous. Benton and the rest of the men were just a little too straight-faced whenever they glanced at him.

The Brigadier winced as Huckle's fist thumped the table yet again. "Three rigs gone in a month. My company's losing millions."

"I assure you, Mr. Huckle, the Government is as concerned as you are."

"If this keeps up there won't be a man willing to work out there . . ." Huckle broke off as a particularly loud wail from the bagpipes drowned his words. "Do we have to put up with that hullaballoo?"

A tall soldier in the uniform of a Warrant Officer entered the little parlor. The Brigadier turned to him thankfully.

"Mr. Benton, any news of the Doctor?"

"Sorry, sir. Not a thing."

Huckle scowled at the interruption. "Who's the Doctor then?"

"Our Scientific Adviser. He ought to have materialized by now."

The Brigadier glanced at the Doctor's calling device. "Is this thing still working, Benton?"

"Far as I know, sir."

A further shuddering wail from upstairs

made the Brigadier put a hand to his temples. "Mr. Benton, please see if you can prevail upon our host to practice the bagpipes when we are out."

Benton grinned and turned to leave. At the window he paused. "Look sir, there's the Doctor now!"

As Benton left the room the Brigadier looked out of the window to see the Doctor, Sarah and Harry climbing out of a muddy station wagon. He turned to Huckle. "Who's that at the wheel?"

Huckle scowled. "That is the Duke of Forgill. Owns pretty well everything around here, except our shore base. He doesn't care for us one little bit."

Seconds later the Doctor breezed into the room, Sarah, Harry and the Duke trailing behind. The Brigadier tried to conceal his relief at seeing him again. "Welcome back, Doctor," he said curtly.

The Doctor, who had no inhibitions about showing his feelings, slapped the Brigadier on the back, shook him warmly by the hand and said, "Hello, Brigadier, hello. I say, I do like the local garb. Suits you, you know, suits you very well." He gazed admiringly at the Brigadier's kilt.

The Brigadier *harrumphed*, and said, "Thank you, Doctor," in an embarrassed way.

Sarah kept her face straight with a mighty effort. She didn't dare look at Harry.

9

"This is His Grace the Duke of Forgill," she said. "He very kindly gave us a lift."

The Duke acknowledged the Brigadier's greeting with formal politeness, but it was obvious that the oil man was the one who really interested him. "I'm glad to have found you here, Mr. Huckle," he said grimly. "It's saved me a trip to your base. I'm afraid I have to complain once more about the behavior of the roughnecks who work for you. They've been trespassing on my property again, and poaching too!"

Huckle reddened with anger but controlled himself with an effort. Unfortunately, he knew there was probably some truth in the Duke's charges. The men who worked for him were a tough, hard-bitten lot. If they fancied a bit of shooting or fishing on their days off, they weren't likely to let a few antiquated game laws stand in their way. "I'm sorry to hear that, your Grace," he spoke with forced politeness. "My men *have* been warned. If any of them are caught, they'll be discharged immediately."

"Then let me add a warning of my own. If my gamekeeper finds any of your men trespassing, they won't be prosecuted—they'll be shot. And I assure you that's not an idle threat, Mr. Huckle."

Huckle didn't trust himself to reply. He turned to the Brigadier and said, "I'll be expecting you at the base then, Brigadier," and marched out of the room.

The Duke looked sternly at the Brigadier. "I trust the Army isn't going to help these oil people. Is that why you've been sent here?"

"No, sir. We're part of a special investigation team."

"Investigating what?" There was a kind of unconscious arrogance in the Duke's voice. He and his family have ruled here for so long, thought Sarah, they can't imagine things changing.

The Brigadier's reply was respectful but firm. "I'm afraid I can't disclose that, sir. Our mission is of a rather confidential nature."

"My family," said the Duke coldly, "has served Scotland for well over seven centuries. That doesn't seem to count for much today. I'll leave you to your official secrets." With a nod of farewell he stumped off. They heard him calling out, "Angus, where are you, man? I've a wee gift for you in the boot of my car. Come and help me carry it!"

"Odd sort of chap," remarked the Brigadier. "Bit medieval in his ideas."

"Well, at least he's a man of conviction," said the Doctor. He suddenly remembered his grievance. "Now then, Brigadier, why did you bring me back? I trust you have a good reason!"

The Brigadier gave him a brief report of the trouble off the Scottish coast. Recently, a large number of offshore oil rigs had been set up to drill for North Sea oil. In the past few weeks three of them had been totally destroyed,

11

smashed into the sea by some incredible force.

The Doctor gazed at the Brigadier indignantly. "Just a minute, Brigadier, just a minute! Do you mean to say you've dragged me back seventeen million miles for this? When I left you the syonic beam I expressly said it was only to be used in an emergency."

"Doctor, this *is* an emergency!"

"Oil, an emergency?" said the Doctor disdainfully. "It's high time this planet ceased to be so dependent on a mineral slime. If you ask me . . ."

"Just one moment!" There was an edge to the Brigadier's voice that silenced even the Doctor. "It isn't only a question of the oil, though I won't deny that's important. These rigs carry a large crew. So far three rigs have been destroyed—and there have been no survivors. Don't you think we ought to solve this mystery before more men die?"

For a moment the two men glared at each other, while Sarah and Harry stood forgotten, holding their breath. Then the Doctor spoke in a very different tone. "Yes, of course," he said. "You were quite right to send for me."

One thing about the Doctor, thought Sarah, he never bothered about saving face. When he was wrong he admitted it, and went on from there.

The Doctor rubbed his hands together briskly and looked around the room. "Right then," he said. "Where do we start?"

2

Murder on the Shore

They started, after a large and filling lunch, with a visit to the shore base of the oil company. This was a small cluster of ultra-modern buildings, huddled together on a bleak stretch of Scottish coastline. Mr. Huckle was obviously overjoyed to see them, if only because it gave him a chance to discuss his worries. In a bright, luxurious, centrally heated office, lined with wall charts and cluttered with communications equipment, he showed them the medical reports on the bodies taken from the sea after each disaster. It was a grim story.

"Exposure and drowning," said Huckle, passing a batch of reports over to Harry Sullivan. "Same cause of death each time."

Harry Sullivan, who had been a Naval doctor before joining UNIT, skimmed rapidly through the reports. "No signs of violence?"

"A few minor injuries, but that's all. Nothing that couldn't have been caused by the sea itself."

"Where are the bodies now?"

Huckle grimaced, "Most of them are still in the local mortuary."

Harry shuffled the papers together. "I'd like to take a look at them, if I may. And I'll need a chance to study these reports in more detail. It may take a little time."

The Brigadier said briskly, "Very well, Sullivan, you cut along. We'll see you back at HQ."

As Harry began to leave, Sarah said, "Wait Harry, I'll come with you as far as the village. I'll interview some of the local people, see if they know anything they're not telling." Sarah was an experienced journalist, and knew that however closely guarded the secret, there was usually someone willing to drop a hint or two, if only to show their own cleverness. If the village people *did* know anything about what was going on, Sarah was sure she could ferret it out.

Sarah and Harry went off. The Doctor didn't even seem to notice them go. He was staring absorbedly at a wall map which showed the position of the company's offshore rigs. Three of them were marked by sinister black crosses. There were many more rigs on the map, unharmed as yet, but obviously in the same danger as those that had vanished.

A model oil rig stood on Huckle's desk. The Brigadier picked it up and examined it curiously. "These things always remind me of spiders in Wellington boots."

Huckle took the model from him. "Correction, Brigadier—spiders in *concrete* boots," he said firmly. "Thousands of tons of it. These rigs are supposed to be unsinkable."

"That's what they said about the *Bismarck*," said the Doctor. "And we all know what happened there! Have you considered seismic disturbance—an undersea earthquake?"

Huckle pointed to the markings which showed the estimated size of the oilfield. "We spent a fortune proving the Waverly Field geologically sound. Everything is constantly checked for stability. Winds, currents, the slightest movement of the sea bed, all charted and recorded. Our instruments showed nothing."

The Doctor wandered across to the elaborate RT set that stood in one corner. "And before every disaster there was a complete radio blackout?"

"That's right. Either there was nothing on the set, or all we got was a sort of electronic burble."

"No other craft in the vicinity? Nothing suspicious?"

"Difficult to be sure," said Huckle frankly. "After all, it was at night. As far as we know, the sea was calm and empty."

"Correction, Mr. Huckle," the Doctor mimicked Huckle's phrase of a moment before. "The sea may be calm—but it's never empty."

Even as the Doctor spoke a vast dark shape was slipping through the sea, heading toward its next target—another oil rig.

* * *

Sarah Jane Smith spent a sociable afternoon chatting to as many people as she could in the little village of Tulloch. It was hard going at first. The village people were polite enough, but they tended to be reserved, unwilling to open up to a stranger. But Sarah had got a foot in quite a few doors in her time as a journalist, and she managed to get most of them talking in the end. Now, an hour or so later, she was discussing her harvest of gossip over tea and scones with Angus MacRanald, burly landlord of the Village Inn.

Away from his bagpipes, Angus was pleasant enough, a little on the dour side, but an occasional twinkle in his eye showed that his grimness was mostly an act. Sarah was taking a mischievous delight in showing off how much she had learned.

"And they say in the village that *you're* the seventh son of a seventh son, that you have the second sight!"

Angus gave a noncommittal grunt. "Aye, mebbe. Yon fellow the Doctor now. He looks like a man who could see 'round a corner or two."

Sarah thought there might be something to the story of Angus's powers after all. It hadn't taken him long to spot something unusual about the Doctor. And since answering questions about the Doctor was always a tricky business,

Sarah did her best to change the subject. She glanced around the room and saw a new addition since the morning. Dominating one wall was a vast, many-antlered stag's head, staring down at her with bulbous glassy eyes that seemed almost alive. "That's a fine looking specimen!"

Angus nodded proudly. "Aye, yon's a twelve-pointer. The Duke himself presented it to me this very day."

Sarah nodded, remembering that she'd seen it in the back of the station wagon. "He's a strange man, the Duke, isn't he?"

"He's my hereditary chieftain," Angus sounded reproving. "The MacRanald, Chief of the Clan."

"I'm sorry, I didn't mean to be rude. It's just that—well, after he picked us up he scarcely spoke a word all the way into the village. He seemed so—preoccupied."

Angus sighed. "It's true enough, he's no' the Duke I remember. He's been a different man since the oil people came. All his servants left him, you see. There was more money to be earned at the base. Forgill Castle's an empty, cold-hearted house these days. I havena' set foot there in a long time. I wouldna' care to now, and that's a fact." There was deep sadness in Angus's voice, and Sarah felt a shiver of unease. She looked around the room. She couldn't rid herself of the strangest feeling that she was being watched. She glanced quickly

17

around, but saw only the oddly gleaming eyes of the stag as it gazed indifferently down at her.

Not far away, in a hidden control room, a claw-like hand reached forward to touch a control. Immediately the scene in the inn parlor appeared on a glowing monitor screen. The alien hand touched another control, and the voices of Sarah and Angus came through, faint but clear.

Sarah shivered and looked away from the stag's head. "Mr. MacRanald, is it true you predicted disaster for the oil company? They say in the village you had a vision."

"Och, I wouldn't say a vision. No more than a wee feeling. They built their base on Tulloch Moor, do you see, and that's a place of bad luck." His voice deepened. "It's a strange murky place, the moor. Its mists are like the steam from a witch's cauldron. Nobody from these parts will cross it after dark."

"Surely that's only superstition?"

"Call it that if you like," said Angus darkly. "But I tell you something. There was once a man staying at this very inn. He went off for a walk on the moor one night and was never seen again."

Sarah's journalistic instincts were aroused. "Sounds like a good story—when did it happen?"

"1922," said Angus solemnly. "Then there was the business of the Jamieson boys. Went cutting peat on the moor. The mist came down

18

and they were benighted. Donald just disappeared. . . . They found his brother Robert two days later. He was clean off his head, and the fear in his eyes was terrible to see."

Sarah couldn't help being impressed. "And when did all this happen?"

"Well it *was* a wee while ago," admitted Angus. "Around 1870, I think."

Sarah laughed, but Angus's voice was utterly serious. "Aye, you may laugh, lassie. But take my word, there are evil spirits haunting Tulloch Moor."

Sarah rose to leave. "That's as maybe. But I'm sure of one thing, Mr. MacRanald—evil spirits don't smash up oil rigs."

Sarah went off to her room to wash and rest. As she left the parlor the glassy eyes of the stag's head seemed to follow her.

The alien hand in the control room reached out, and the monitor screen clicked into darkness.

The mist from the sea drifted in over Tulloch Moor, blurring the outlines of the gorse and the few stunted trees, making the moor seem more eerie and sinister than ever. A huge figure came striding through the mist, and a nervous villager might easily have taken it for some ghoul or goblin out of Angus MacRanald's stories. But a closer glance would have brought reassurance. It was only the Caber, faithful game-

19

keeper, servant and companion of the Duke of Forgill. Everyone in Tulloch knew the Caber. Indeed it was impossible to mistake him. A champion of the Highland Games, his massive size had caused one of the judges to remark that he was as big as a "caber," the trimmed tree trunk that he was tossing. The name had stuck, and the Duke's ghillie had been called the Caber ever since.

One thing about the Caber might have puzzled the villagers, if there had been anyone on the moor to see him—the gun in the crook of his arm. There was nothing strange about the Caber having a gun. But this wasn't the old, well-cared-for shotgun he usually carried. This was something else altogether. Resting in the crook of the Caber's arm was a heavy, big-game rifle with telescopic sight.

The sea mist was thickest at the water's edge. It swirled around what looked like a huge, humped piece of driftwood that had floated in on the incoming tide. For a moment it lay there, a shapeless lump. Then the "hump" slowly detached itself, and took on the shape of a man. Jock Munro let go of the piece of wood that had saved his life and began crawling up the beach. He had floated for untold hours in the freezing sea, and now his instinct was to get away from it. Crawling at first, and then in a shambling, staggering run, he made his way toward the road.

The mist drifted in patches across the road,

coming and going with amazing rapidity. It made driving a tricky business, and Harry Sullivan had no wish to pile up his borrowed oil company landrover. He drove slowly and carefully, keeping speed down to a minimum. Even so, he had to step hard on the brakes when a shapeless figure lurched out from the mist and collapsed in front of him. The landrover's front wheels stopped only a few feet from the body as Harry jumped out and knelt beside it. The man's clothes, hair, even his skin itself, were soggy with water. Harry guessed instinctively that this was a survivor of one of the wrecked oil rigs, and the briefest examination told him that, unless he got warmth, shelter, and dry clothing, the man wasn't going to survive much longer. He started to drag the body carefully toward the landrover. To his amazement the survivor stirred and began to mutter, "The rig . . . I was on the rig."

"All right, old chap," said Harry soothingly. "We'll soon get you to a hospital."

Munro shook his head. "I'm thinking you're too late."

The feeble voice and the faint flickering of his pulse convinced Harry the man might well be right. He put reassurance into his voice. "No, you'll be all right. Can you tell me what happened to the rig?"

"Didn't stand a chance . . . came at us suddenly . . ." The voice trailed away.

"What did?" asked Harry urgently. "What came at you?"

The Caber settled himself on the hilltop, face down in the gorse, legs spread for balance, elbows forming a steady tripod. He cuddled the walnut stock of the gun into his shoulder and peered through the telescopic sight. The two figures on the road below sprang up in sharp relief. He moved the rifle barrel steadily until the cross-hairs of the telescopic sight intersected on his target . . .

Harry put his head closer to Munro's, trying to pick out the sense of the feeble words. He was reluctant to delay getting the man to a hospital, but those mutterings could contain a vital clue, and if the journey *was* too much for the poor chap . . . "Huge . . . terrible . . ." Munro was saying faintly. "Charged again and again. Smashed the rig to pieces . . .

Munro's body jerked, and was twitched from Harry's arms as if by a giant invisible hand. Too astonished to move, Harry saw blood gush from the wound in the man's chest. The rifle boomed again and Harry spun around, his hand clutching his head, and collapsed across Munro.

The sea mist swirled slowly around the two motionless bodies.

3

The Zygons Attack

When Sarah came down from her room, UNIT's temporary HQ was empty except for the Doctor. He was happily fiddling with a pile of electronic equipment which he had spread all over the big table. Sarah peered over his shoulder. "What's all this then?"

The Doctor sighed. Sarah's constant curiosity about anything and everything was one of her most engaging characteristics, but it could get a little wearing. He knew from experience it was no good trying to put her off. Only a clear, precise explanation would satisfy that enquiring journalistic mind. He spoke without looking up from his work. "This is part of a probe system for detecting localized jamming and alien energy emissions."

Sarah considered for a moment and said, "What happens if whatever's doing the jamming jams the jamming detector?"

The Doctor opened his mouth to deliver a crushing reply, then realized with a shock that Sarah was quite right. He'd overlooked that problem. "I shall build in a protective circuit," he said with dignity, hurriedly assembling the necessary parts.

Sarah started wandering around the room. She wanted to tell the Doctor about her chats with Angus and the villagers, but he was obviously too preoccupied to listen. She glanced up, met the baleful glare of the stag's head, and hurriedly looked away. "Where's the Brigadier?"

"Down at the quayside, I think. They're bringing in some wreckage from one of the rigs. I asked him to get the stuff to me here before too many people know about it."

"No use trying to be secretive in this village," said Sarah darkly. "The landlord's got the second sight."

The Doctor made a minute adjustment to a very small circuit. "Maybe we should recruit him into UNIT."

The telephone rang, and Sarah picked it up. It was the Brigadier, and his news made Sarah go pale with shock.

She said, "Yes, he's here, I'll tell him. We'll come at once."

Something in her voice made the Doctor look up. "What is it, Sarah? Bad news?"

Sarah nodded. "It's Harry—he's been shot!"

The hidden control room was filled with a strange sound. It was a high-pitched electronic gurgling, rhythmic and monotonous. The creature at the console reached out, touched one of the nodules on the control panel, and the noise went up in pitch.

The control console, and indeed the entire control room, was as peculiar and alien in shape as the creatures operating it. It was made of a strange, gnarled, fibrous material, and somehow seemed to have been grown rather than constructed. Instead of knobs and levers there were root-like stumps and projections, while sensitive nodules replaced buttons and switches.

The alien being at the console was a Zygon. Its name was Broton, and its voice when it spoke had a hissing, gurlging quality, curiously like the noise that filled the air. "What is the impulse strength?"

On the other side of the control room, another Zygon presided over a similar bank of root-like instruments. It replied in the same hissing, gurgling tones. "Diastellic reading seven-o-three."

"Increase the sonic call tone by three remars," Broton ordered.

The Zygon's claw-like hands moved obediently over the control nodules. "Increased tone, three remars. Contact firm."

"Check directional pulse."

"Pulse correct to within one Earth mile. Closing."

"Adjust final course for target strike."

The subordinate Zygon touched more control nodules. Miles away, in the chill depths of the sea, a huge, powerful shape altered its course a few degrees, responding to the alien hands that controlled its movements.

In his office at the oil company base, Huckle crouched over his RT set. He spent every available moment on the air these days, checking and re-checking that the rest of the steel giants for which he was responsible still stood securely on the ocean bed. Every transmission he made was a fresh ordeal; each time he dreaded that the rig he was calling would not reply. He crouched tensely over the set. "Do you read me, Ben Nevis, do you read me?"

There was silence, except for the crackle of static. Then, "Hibernian Control, this is Ben Nevis rig, over."

Huckle gave a sigh of relief. Without realizing it, he'd been holding his breath. "Got you, Ben Nevis, loud and clear."

In the radio room of Ben Nevis rig, the operator grinned sympathetically. He knew Huckle well, and realized what he must be going through. Huckle's voice crackled from the set.

"How are you doing out there? How's morale?"

The operator felt like asking, "What morale?" After three disasters the rig crews were in a state of near mutiny, and only the promise of huge danger bonuses kept them working at all.

26

Restraining himself, the operator said, "Could be worse. Any news of the investigation?"

"Not much. This Brigadier chap's brought in his Scientific Adviser. Weird fellow called the Doctor. He seems . . ."

Huckle's voice was cut off in mid-sentence. A strange electronic burbling came from the set. The operator at Ben Nevis rig flicked switches and adjusted dials, but all in vain. He switched to transmitting. "Hallo, Hibernian Control, we seem to have lost you. Are you still reading me? Over."

There was no reply, only the electronic sound which was getting louder and louder. Suddenly the entire cabin reeled as some huge object struck the rig a massive blow. Thrown from his chair, the operator struck his head against one of the steel walls, and slumped unconscious to the floor. The strange electronic burble filled the little cabin, rising higher and higher.

The sound was filling Huckle's office too, as he flicked frantically at the controls. "Ben Nevis, Ben Nevis, are you there? Over." There was no reply.

Huckle abandoned the RT set, grabbed his phone and sent out a general alarm. Within minutes he heard the sound of company helicopters taking off. But there was no hope in Huckle's face as he slumped down behind his desk. He already knew what they would find— nothing. An empty place in the sea where an oil rig had once stood.

* * *

Harry Sullivan lay white and motionless in one of the oil company's sick-bay beds, a bandage around his head. The Doctor looked at the neat figure of Sister Lamont, who hovered by the bed. "Has he spoken at all?"

There was a soft Highland lilt in the nurse's voice. "Not a word, I'm afraid. The wound on his skull is no more than a graze, but he's still in shock."

The Doctor leaned over. "Harry, it's me, the Doctor. Can you hear me?"

Harry stirred and mumbled. He seemed to be trying to speak.

The Brigadier rushed in, stopped, and looked down at the bandaged figure. "How is he? Will he be all right, Sister?"

"He'll be fine. He just needs to rest."

The Brigadier remembered his news. "Doctor, they've lost another rig, the Ben Nevis. Forty men aboard. It's completely vanished."

"Same pattern as before?"

"Exactly. Same radio blackout, same burbling sound . . ."

"Did you bring that wreckage from the other rig for me?"

"It's all back at HQ now. Though what you think you'll learn from a pile of metal junk . . ."

"I'd better get to work." The Doctor made for the door, the Brigadier close behind him.

Sarah didn't move. "I'll stay with Harry for a while. I can let you know if he wakes up!"

The Doctor paused in the doorway. "Good idea, Sarah. I think he'll soon be coming 'round. If he can talk, he may be able to tell us something."

As the two men went down the corridor, Sarah could hear the Brigadier's voice. "I hope you can come up with *something* to show Huckle, Doctor. He's coming down to HQ for a conference later on, and he's hopping mad."

"My dear Brigadier, the purpose of my experiments is *not* to satisfy Mr. Huckle, but to discover the truth. He'll just have to be patient and so will you. . . ."

Their voices died away and Sarah looked again at Harry. He was still muttering and twisting, and seemed to be trying to speak. She leaned close. "Harry, it's Sarah. Can you hear me?"

Sister Lamont came quickly forward. "I really think you should let him rest. He *is* under sedation, you know. Perhaps if you come back later?"

Sarah's voice was polite, but quite determined. "I think I'll stay if you don't mind. I'd like to be here when he wakes." She sat back in her chair, watching Harry's face.

The Doctor's electronic tracing equipment had been set up in one corner of the room, and a UNIT signals technician was manning it. Now the big table was occupied by packets of white powder, buckets and bowls of water, and a pile of chunks of twisted metal—part of the wreckage from a destroyed rig. More wreckage was piled in a corner. Working with quiet concentration, the Doctor was chipping delicately at a chunk of hardened white plaster. He was so absorbed that he didn't look up when the Brigadier brought Huckle into the room.

The Brigadier coughed, and when this had no response he said heartily, "Well, as you can see, Mr. Huckle, the Doctor's hard at work."

Huckle didn't seem over-impressed. "Do you mind telling us exactly what you're doing, Doctor?"

The Doctor continued his chipping. "A little experiment in orthodontology."

"Orthodontology?" It was clear from Huckle's tone that he was none the wiser.

"Teeth, Mr. Huckle," said the Doctor sharply. "The scientific study of teeth!" He chipped away the last few flakes of plaster, and held up the finished result. "This is the plaster cast of a tooth, don't you agree?"

And indeed it was—a tooth of enormous size. It reminded Huckle of the reconstructions of dinosaur teeth he'd seen in museums. "Are you trying to tell me my rigs were *chewed* up—by a set of molars?"

The Doctor's voice was thoughtful. "It would

be more correct to say dentures. Made of some material that can cut through concrete and steel like paper."

This was too much for the Brigadier. "Come on now, Doctor. First you suggest we're dealing with some kind of sea monster, then you say it's got false teeth."

The Doctor stood up, brushing flakes of plaster from his clothes. "We're certainly dealing with a kind of monster," he agreed. "Something of frightening size and power. But this is no ordinary sea serpent. It's a creature whose natural power and strength has been boosted by artificial means. We're dealing with a cyborg, something part-animal and part-machine!"

In the Zygon control room, Broton switched off his monitor screen with a hiss of rage. "This one they call the Doctor is a threat to us. Already he has discovered too much. *He must be killed!*"

Sarah's long vigil at Harry's bedside was rewarded at last. Harry opened his eyes, smiled at her and said, "Sarah . . ." His voice was weak, but perfectly clear. "Could I have something to drink, please?"

Sarah poured a glass of water and held it to his lips. He swallowed thirstily and said, "Sarah, listen . . . got to tell you . . ." His voice tailed away, his strength suddenly gone.

"Harry, what is it? What are you trying to

31

say . . ." Sarah looked up as Sister Lamont came quickly into the room. "Sister, he's coming around."

Sister Lamont leaned over the bed, smoothing Harry's pillow and making him more comfortable. As his eyes opened again, Sarah said, "What did you find out, Harry? The man who was killed, did he tell you anything?"

Harry frowned, obviously making a mighty effort. "He said the rig was shaking . . . falling. Then . . . he saw . . ." The effort was too much, and he slumped back on his pillow.

Sarah jumped up. "Will you stay with him, Sister? I've got to ring the Doctor. And please, be sure to remember anything he says. It could be very important."

As Sarah ran from the room, Sister Lamont bent over the bed, the soothing Highland lilt in her voice. "It's all right, Dr. Sullivan, you're quite safe. You're going to be well looked after."

Harry looked up at the figure leaning over him. Suddenly it seemed to blur and change. His eyes widened and he screamed, "No . . . No!" An alien hand clamped across his mouth, cutting off his voice.

On the telephone in the corridor, Sarah poured out her news. The Doctor's voice was cheerful and reassuring.

"He's coming around and seems quite rational? That's splendid! Keep an eye on him, I'll be over as soon as I can. Oh, and, Sarah, get the sick bay people to keep his recovery dark. Let everyone think he's still out cold, eh? Might be safer."

"Safer You mean Harry's still in danger from . . ."

A hand came down on Sarah's shoulder. But it wasn't a human hand. It was orange-green in color, claw-like and alien. It was the hand of a Zygon.

4

A Trap for the Doctor

Sarah swung around. Facing her was a squat, powerful figure about the size of a small man. Orange-green in color, it had small, claw-like hands and feet. There was no neck: the big high-domed head seemed to grow directly from the bulbous torso. The face was terrifyingly alien, with huge, malevolent green eyes and a small, puckered mouth. A row of protuberances ran down its back. The really horrible thing about the creature was that it seemed to be a parody of the human form. It looked like a grotesque, evil baby.

Sarah opened her mouth to scream, but even as she drew breath the creature reached out and grabbed her with its claw. A force like a massive electric shock slammed Sarah against the wall, and she slid unconscious to the floor.

At UNIT HQ the Doctor spoke into the phone, "Sarah? Sarah, can you hear me?" There was no answer. He slammed down the receiver and turned to Benton. "Something's happened to Sarah. We'd better get over that at once."

Thanks to some spectacular driving by the

Doctor, they arrived in an amazingly short time. They rushed into the sick bay to find Harry's bed empty, no sign of Sarah, and Sister Lamont fluttering about in a state of great agitation. "I assure you, gentlemen, I was only gone a few minutes. Dr. Sullivan began to talk, you see, and Miss Smith went off to call you. I waited and waited, and when she didn't come back, I was worried and went to look for her. I couldn't find her anywhere—and when I got back, Dr. Sullivan had gone too."

"Maybe he woke up delirious, and wandered off somewhere," said Benton. "I'll get some men over and search the area."

The Doctor nodded thoughtfully. "It's possible—but what happened to Sarah? Sister Lamont, will you show me this telephone she used?"

While Benton used his walkie-talkie to contact UNIT, Sister Lamont led the Doctor along the spotless white corridor to a telephone fixed to the wall. "When I came along the telephone was just swinging on its cord. I thought it odd at the time."

"Nobody else was on duty?"

"No. We're just a small establishment here."

The Doctor stood quite still, apparently lost in thought. He nodded toward a door further down the corridor. "Where does that lead?"

"It's a decompression unit. We sometimes need it for the company divers. But it's always kept locked." Sister Lamont seemed struck by a sudden thought. "You know, I've just remembered, I haven't looked in the dispensary." She hurried off in the other direction.

Left to himself, the Doctor wandered across to the decompression unit. Almost idly he tried the door. It swung open as soon as he touched it, and he went inside.

He found himself in a kind of antechamber. Set into one wall was a huge metal door, a big locking-wheel in its center. Higher in the door was a small observation window, covered by a Venetian blind. He crossed to the window and peered through the chinks. The decompression chamber was small, bare, featureless. Sarah lay unconscious in the middle of the floor.

Swiftly the Doctor spun the locking wheel, hauled open the door and climbed into the chamber. Kneeling by Sarah, he lifted her head and shoulders. Sarah's eyes snapped open, and she parted her lips to scream in blind panic. The Doctor shook her gently. "It's all right, Sarah. It's me."

Sarah shook her head confusedly. "Doctor? I was talking to you on the telephone—then I saw this . . . thing." She struggled to sit up. "What about Harry? Is he all right?"

"I'm afraid he's disappeared."

"Oh, no . . ." Suddenly she broke off. "Doctor—look!" The heavy metal door of the decompression chamber was swinging closed. The Doctor sprang across the room, just too late to stop it. On the other side of the door, two claw-

37

like alien hands were turning the wheel. The hands touched controls on a nearby panel; there was a low hum as the needles on the dials jumped to life. A gauge that registered the pressure of air in the chamber began dropping steadily . . .

Sarah and the Doctor listened to the low hum.

"What's that noise?" Sarah asked nervously. "Some kind of air conditioning?"

The Doctor was examining the observation window. As he feared, it was made of reinforced glass, impossible to break. "I'm afraid not, Sarah. In fact, just the reverse."

Sarah swung around, suddenly becoming fully aware of her surroundings. "Where are we? What is this place?"

"It's a decompression chamber." The Doctor went on examining the door. He patted his pockets for his sonic screwdriver. If there was time he could use the laser attachment to cut their way out, or at least make an air hole for them.

Sarah tried to remember what she knew about decompression chambers. Sometimes divers had to come up too quickly because of some emergency. If that happened, the abrupt change in pressure could be dangerous, and they had to spend time in a decompression chamber, to enable their bodies to adjust. Presumably a decompression chamber was basically a sealed space where you could vary the air pressure . . .

Sarah felt suddenly dizzy. She tried breathing deeply, but it didn't help. She tugged the Doctor's sleeve. "Doctor—I can't breathe. There doesn't seem to be any air in here."

The Doctor went on working frantically. The specially hardened glass of the window was incredibly tough, and even the sonic screwdriver seemed to make very little impression. "Sarah, sit perfectly still. Try to save your breath."

Sarah sat slumped against the wall, breathing shallowly. "They're pumping the air out, aren't they? We're going to die!" She felt oddly detached, as if this were all happening to someone else.

The Doctor looked at her worriedly, trying to remember human reaction to oxygen deprivation. Unconscious in two minutes, dead in under ten, wasn't that it? He realized he simply could not get through the door in time to save Sarah's life. Or his own for that matter. His resistance was far greater than Sarah's, but lack of oxygen would kill them both in the end. Unless . . . unless . . .

He crossed over to Sarah and sat down beside her. "Sarah, look at me—and listen. Concentrate—look into my eyes." Muzzily, Sarah obeyed. The Doctor's face swung before her, seeming to get nearer and farther, larger and smaller. She was conscious only of his burning eyes, and his urgent hypnotic voice. "Listen to me, Sarah. You do not *need* to breathe. You feel nothing, nothing, nothing . . ." The final word seemed to echo inside Sarah's head as blackness swallowed her up.

Outside in the corridor, the Zygon that had worn the shape of Sister Lamont spoke into a small communications device. There was a note of gloating triumph in its voice. "The trap has been sprung. The Doctor and the human female will soon be dead."

The message was received by Broton in his control room. "Excellent," he said, in tones of equal satisfaction, and looked down scornfully at the wounded human slumped by his feet.

Harry Sullivan recovered consciousness slowly, and felt that he had wakened into a nightmare. Vague memories floated into his head. The man he'd found by the roadside . . . being in bed, the Doctor and Sarah looking down at him, then that nurse—and now this. He was in a kind of fantastic control room where nightmarish creatures moved about mysterious tasks. The whole place seemed alive in some weird fashion all of its own. The fibrous walls were broken up with strange protuberances, odd-shaped nodules and roots, and there were glowing veins in walls and ceilings, and tangles of fibrous roots and vines running everywhere. Somehow the place looked as if it had been *grown* rather than made.

The after-effects of Harry's wound had left him feeling curiously lightheaded. Perhaps it *was* all a nightmare, he concluded. Maybe he was still tucked up in bed, with Sarah and the Doctor waiting for him to wake up.

Still, nightmare or not, he decided there was no reason why he shouldn't find out where he was. He struggled to his feet and tapped the nearest creature on the shoulder. "I say, what in the name of blazes *are* you?"

The Zygon spun around, hissing malevolently. "I am Broton, Warlord of the Zygons. It is a name you will learn to fear, human."

Harry was struck by the note of colossal arrogance in the voice. Whatever these weird things were, they certainly thought a lot of themselves.

"Who are you? Where do you come from?"

Broton glared angrily at him, tempted to blast down this insolent human. Then it struck him that it might be amusing to overawe this primitive creature with the might of Zygon technology, to see his fear when he knew the fate that awaited his planet. Broton spoke slowly in his hissing, gurgling voice. "Centuries ago, by your Time scale, our craft was damaged. We landed here and concealed ourselves. Over the long years we regenerated, regained our former strength. But when the subspace communicator was at last repaired, we received terrible news. Our world was destroyed in a stellar explosion. The survivors roam the galaxy in their spaceships, exiles like ourselves. We can never return home."

41

For a moment Harry was touched by the sadness in the creature's voice. But any trace of sympathy vanished with Broton's next words. "Since our planet is no more, we must make *this* planet our own. All resistance will be crushed. We shall change the destiny of Earth!" The voice rose to a high, triumphant shriek.

Broton looked expectantly at Harry, waiting to see him collapse in terror. To his disappointment the human seemed totally unimpressed.

"I seem to have heard that one before," said Harry. "How do you propose to set about it?"

Broton gave a hiss of rage. He pressed one of the control nodules and a screen slid back to reveal a long observation window. Harry peered through it, and saw with a shock that the window looked out into murky, swirling water. Broton pressed another nodule, and a low electronic burbling filled the room. "Look, human," he ordered.

Obediently, Harry looked. For a moment or two he saw nothing. Then he gasped in astonishment. A huge shape had loomed up, and was drifting slowly by the window. Harry stared in amazement at the fierce head on the immensely long neck, the huge body with its two low humps, the two pairs of flippers front and rear, and the flat, powerful tail. "We must be under Loch Ness," gasped Harry. "And that thing— that's the monster!"

"To us, human, it is the Skarasen. A native of

our planet—and in your terminology, our ultimate weapon!"

Broton touched a control. The noise died down and the monster swam away. The cover slid back over the window. Harry shook his head wonderingly. "How did you manage to bring a thing that size with you?"

"As an embryo. It was grown and reared here on your planet. The Skarasen is our life source. We Zygons need its lactic fluid to survive."

So the monster was also a kind of milk-cow, thought Harry. He blurted out his next thought before he could stop himself. "Then if that thing is killed, you die too?"

"None of your human weapons can affect the Skarasen. Our technology is supreme."

"Ours isn't so bad either," Harry said defiantly. "I doubt if your little pet would survive a nuclear missile."

"The merest pin-prick," Broton was scornful. "We have converted the Skarasen into a cyborg of devastating power. Nothing can stand against the Zygons. Nothing!"

Suddenly Broton tired of his sport. The human was failing to show the proper reactions. He should have been pleading for mercy by now. "Take him away and prepare him, " he ordered. Another Zygon stepped up behind Harry and seized his arms in a powerful grip.

Harry realized he had forgotten to ask the most important question of all. "What about *me*?" he yelled. "Why have you brought me here?"

As he was dragged struggling from the control room, Harry heard Broton's mocking reply. "We have brought you here, human, because we need your body."

5

The Sleeping Village

The Brigadier was feeling aggrieved. Not for the first time, he brooded over the tendency of his assistants to disappear just when needed. Harry was missing. Sarah was missing. The Doctor and Benton had gone off to look for them, and now *they* were missing. For want of anything better to do, the Brigadier started harrying his HQ staff.

"Is the cordon set up on the moor?"

"Yes, sir," said Corporal Palmer patiently.

"Remember now," snapped the Brigadier, "I want a twenty-four-hour watch kept on every inch of this coastline."

Corporal Palmer sighed. He'd already set up liaison with Trinity House, the Coastguard and the Royal Navy. However, he refrained from pointing this out to the Brigadier, contenting himself with a brisk, efficient, "Sir!" as he got on with his work.

The Brigadier studied a map of the coastline. "If the Doctor's right, and some kind of sea monster is attacking the rigs, we've got to be ready for anything."

"Sir!" said Palmer again, thinking they'd all be ready a lot sooner if the Brigadier would clear off and let them get on with it.

A new and alarming thought struck the Brigadier. "The thing might decide to come inland somewhere else, and bypass our cordon. You'd better warn the local police to be on the alert."

"Sir!" said Palmer. He'd seen to all that half an hour ago.

The Brigadier regarded him with some irritation. The super-efficient Palmer was invaluable, but it was possible to be *too* efficient. "Can't you say anything else but 'Sir!'?" he demanded irritably.

"Sorry, sir!" The RT operator passed Palmer a message slip and he seized thankfully on the diversion. "Message from Sergeant Fletcher's squad, sir. They've arrived at McNab Point and set up a listening watch with some of that new equipment of the Doctor's. So far they say there's . . ."

Palmer's voice slowed, his eyes glazed, and he slid gently to the floor.

The Brigadier stared at him in utter disbelief. Sleeping on duty was a serious offence in itself, but actually dropping off under the eye of a superior officer . . . "Corporal Palmer!" he barked, "Get a grip of yourself, man." Palmer made no reply. He seemed to be fast alseep. The Brigadier turned to his orderly clerk.

"Look after the Corporal. He seems to have . . ." The Brigadier's voice tailed away. The

46

clerk was dozing peacefully, his head buried in a pile of report forms. The RT operator was sprawled across his set. *Everyone* in the room was asleep—and a thin mist was seeping under the door and spreading through the place. The Brigadier rushed to the door and flung it open. A thicker cloud of the same mist billowed into the room, and the Brigadier slumped to the floor.

The room was silent, except for the sound of heavy breathing and the occasional snore. After a moment the telephone began to ring, but there was no one to answer it.

In the sick-bay corridor, Warrant Officer Benton listened to the ringing at the other end of the line in utter amazement. It was impossible that there should be no answer. Whatever the crisis, they'd always leave someone to man the communications.

He slammed down the receiver as his men came along the corridor. "No sign of the Doctor?"

"No, sir."

Benton sighed in exasperation. "Now we've got *three* missing! Not to mention the whole of HQ." Like the Brigadier before him, Benton began to feel the victim of a mass disappearing act. A search of the grounds had revealed no trace of Sarah or Harry. And on returning to the sick bay, they'd found that the Doctor and Sister Lamont had also vanished. Benton turned to the puzzled soldiers. "Come on, we'd better search the building. You go that way, I'll take a look in here."

Purely by chance, the door Benton chose was the one leading to the decompression chamber. He looked briefly round the anteroom, and was just about to leave when he saw the heavy metal door and the little window with its Venetian blind. Casually he walked across and peered in. What he saw made him give a yell that brought the UNIT soldiers running back. Sarah and the Doctor were sitting cross-legged against the far wall of the little chamber. Both were as still as death.

Benton spun the locking-wheel frantically, and heaved at the door. It wouldn't budge. The soldiers joined in to help, but the door resisted their combined strength.

Benton studied the control panel by the door, and swiftly adjusted controls. He watched the air-pressure climb steadily and said, "All right—let's try again." They heaved on the door and slowly it gave way. Benton climbed into the chamber and crossed to the Doctor. He sat completely still, stiff and corpse-like. Despairingly Benton wondered if rigor mortis had already set in. Then, suddenly one of the Doctor's eyes flicked open. It stared unwinkingly at Benton for a moment, then the other eye opened.

The Doctor's nose twitched, he sneezed, and then took in a great gulp of the air flooding into the chamber. A delighted grin spread over his face. "It worked."

Benton gave a sigh of relief. "*What* worked?"

"Oh, just an old trick I learned from a Tibetan monk," said the Doctor airily. He saw a soldier trying to revive Sarah and called hastily, "Don't touch her. It's fatal to break the trance incorrectly!" The Doctor moved over to Sarah, cupped her face in his hands, and gently stroked her forehead with his thumbs. He applied pressure to carefully selected points in her neck, gave her a hearty slap on the back, and Sarah came to life as if she'd been switched on. For the second time that day, she recovered consciousness to see the Doctor gazing down at her.

"Doctor—what happened?"

"I had to put us both into a kind of suspended animation, so we'd survive long enough to be rescued," the Doctor explained cheerfully. "Congratulations, Sarah. You're a remarkably good subject."

Sarah climbed shakily to her feet. "I'm *so* glad. Do you think we could get out of this place now?"

"What an excellent idea!" agreed the Doctor cheerfully. "You know, I really think we'd better pop along to see the Brigadier—he must be wondering what's happened to us."

"*I'm* wondering what's happening to *him*," said Benton. He explained about the abortive telephone call.

The Doctor looked worried. "We'd better get back right away."

Sarah said suddenly, "What about poor Harry? We've got to find him."

The Doctor's voice was reassuring. "I think he's a prisoner of the aliens. When we find their base, we'll rescue him!"

An astonished Huckle stood looking about him in the middle of UNIT HQ. One of his divers, examining the sunken remains of a wrecked rig, had come up with a very interesting discovery, and Huckle had decided to inform UNIT right away. The last thing he'd expected was to find them literally asleep on the job. Yet all around the Brigadier and his HQ staff were sleeping soundly, impervious to all attempts to wake them.

A strange, eerie feeling began to creep over Huckle. He remembered his drive through the village—he hadn't seen a living soul. He looked about uneasily, wondering what to do next. Suddenly, from out on the moor, came a terrifying sound. Like the bellowing of some enormous beast . . .

One of the Brigadier's patrolling soldiers heard the sound at the same time. He was actually out on the moor, and the noise was very much closer. It made the already terrified soldier cock his rifle, and peer nervously into the impenetrable mist that surrounded him.

He'd been on the moor for several hours now, on the outer limits of the cordon set up by the Brigadier to keep watch for the monster. By rights he should have been relieved some time ago. But his relief hadn't arrived, the sergeant hadn't been round to check up, and his increasingly frantic RT calls to UNIT HQ had received no reply. The sudden shattering roar from out of the mist was too much for him. His nerve broke and he turned to run.

Something huge and powerful was crossing Tulloch Moor, moving, for all its vast bulk, at incredible speed. The fleeing soldier ran right across its path. He caught a fleeting glimpse of the monstrous head on its long neck, and then a massive paw crushed him into the ground. The creature bellowed once more as it disappeared into the mist.

The Doctor, Sarah, and Benton heard the roar just as they arrived at the inn. They dashed into the parlor only to find it full of sleeping soldiers, with a terrified Huckle trying to shake them awake. Benton decided to take a look outside, while the Doctor made a quick examination of the Brigadier and his men. Sarah went off to look around the inn itself. She came back into the parlor as the Doctor finished his examination.

Huckle hovered nervously beside him. "Well, what's the verdict?"

"Nerve gas," explained the Doctor. "Something affecting the higher consciousness to produce all the effects of natural sleep. Concentrated, localized, and extremely powerful."

"Are they going to be all right?"

"Right as rain," said the Doctor cheerfully. "Look, they're starting to come out of it now." And indeed, all round the room, men were stirring and muttering.

Sarah said, "*Everyone* in the place is alseep, Doctor. All the staff, guests . . . everyone."

"I can beat that," said Benton, following her in. "Everyone in the village seems to be asleep. My patrols too, as far as I can tell. No one's answering the RT."

The Doctor seemed unsurprised.

"Why?" demanded Sarah. "Why should anyone want to knock out an entire village full of people?"

Benton agreed. "That's right, Doc—why? Doesn't make any sense."

"It makes sense, all right," said the Doctor. "Someone, or rather *something*, wanted to pass this way unseen."

"The *something* that gave the roar we heard?" asked Huckle.

The Doctor nodded. "Very probably."

Benton made for the door. "I'm going to check on my patrols. Tell the Brig, will you—when he comes to."

The Doctor nodded, and turned to Huckle. "Now then, Mr. Huckle," he said brightly. "What can we do for you?" He sounded for all the world like an old-fashioned shopkeeper welcoming a customer, thought Sarah.

Huckle stared blankly at the Doctor, who said gently, "Did you have some special reason for coming here?"

"Yes—yes of course. My divers were checking what's left of the rigs and one of them found this. It was stuck to the concrete foundations, well below the water line."

Huckle produced a strange-looking object. It might have been a large, old-fashioned hearing aid that had been in the sea long enough to get encrusted with weed and barnacles, thought Sarah. Or it could have been an oddly shaped piece of rock that just happened to look like something manufactured. In fact, though Sarah didn't know it, the thing had the half-made, half-grown look of all Zygon technology.

The Doctor took the device from Huckle almost reverently. Stepping carefully over the sleeping form of the Brigadier, he took it to the table and began to examine it. "You know, Mr. Huckle," he remarked happily, "I think we're getting somewhere at last!"

The Doctor's good spirits were not shared by Broton, Warlord of the Zygons. He stood in his control room hissing with rage at the news brought by one of his subordinates. "You assured me the Doctor and the female were dead.

Now I hear they have arrived safely at the village. Explain!"

The Zygon who had worn the shape of Sister Lamont cringed under Broton's wrath. "I don't understand, Commander. They were dying when I left them."

With a hiss of disgust, Broton turned to the console and touched a control nodule. Once again the scene in the parlor of the inn sprang into view on the monitor screen.

The Doctor was holding up the device Huckle had brought him. "You realize what this is, Mr. Huckle? A calling device!"

"For this monster you reckon's chewing up my rigs?"

"Correct! You've made an invaluable find."

Angrily Broton hissed at the screen, "You are too clever, Doctor—and too dangerous. This time I will make *certain* that you die." He switched off the monitor and strode angrily from the control room.

Somewhere in the depths of the Zygon ship, Harry Sullivan stood motionless in a kind of alcove, shaped rather like an upright coffin. With tentacles, seemingly part of the ship itself, wound around him so he couldn't move. He was in no particular discomfort, and during the long wait sheer boredom had driven away his fear. He looked up almost eagerly when Broton and another Zygon strode up to him. "All right, Broton, you said you wanted my body. Now, what are you going to do with it?"

Again Broton wondered why this primitive being failed to show the proper terrified reaction. Perhaps another demonstration of the all-powerful might of Zygon technology would make him realize his insignificance. "It is not precisely your body that we need, human. It is your body print. That has now been taken, by the Zygon device which imprisons you—a brilliant piece of technology far beyond your understanding."

Broton touched a nearby control nodule, and a section of wall slid back to reveal a row of alcoves, similar to the one holding Harry. In each alcove stood a human body, frozen and motionless, the head partly covered by a transparent dome. Harry saw the Duke of Forgill, Sister Lamont, and several others he didn't recognize, including a huge powerful man in gamekeeper's dress. Harry gazed in horror. "These people—are they all dead?"

"No . . . they live . . . after a fashion."

"Why have you done this to them? What's it all for?"

Broton stepped up to the alcove containing the big gamekeeper. "Watch!" He placed his hand on a panel beside the alcove. The panel glowed and hummed with power. Unbelievingly Harry saw Broton blur and shimmer and *change*. Suddenly a replica of the gamekeeper stood looking at him.

Harry had a sudden vision of the face of Sister Lamont, changing into a Zygon as she stood over his bed in the sick bay.

Horribly, the gamekeeper spoke with Broton's voice, though Harry guessed that the voice could be copied too. "We have the power to rearrange the molecular structure of our bodies, to turn into replicas of your unpleasant species whenever it is necessary." The gamekeeper shimmered, and turned back into Broton.

Harry struggled to keep his voice calm. "I still don't see what use I am to you."

The Zygon with Broton came up to Harry's cubicle, and put his hand on the panel, "Do you not, human? Then watch!"

Just as Broton had, the Zygon began to change. Harry watched. This time there was real fear in his eyes. "No," he cried. "No!" He watched in sheer horror as the Zygon took on its new form.

6

The Monster on the Moor

At UNIT HQ, dazed soldiers were stumbling slowly to their feet. In the middle of the confusion, the Doctor sat quietly contemplating the calling device. There seemed no join, nowhere to get *into* it, and he was reluctant to use force for fear of damaging it.

Sarah looked curiously at the tiny object. "What do you think it's *for*, Doctor?"

"Well, suppose one of these things was clamped to the base of each rig? A long-range signal activates it, and gives some kind of summons—maybe a monster's mating call!"

The Doctor tossed the device up in the air and caught it. "I can learn a great deal from this—but we've got to handle it carefully."

"I should," said Huckle. "If it whistles up that creature we heard bellowing . . ." He shivered. "Is there anything I can do?"

"You've done enough, Mr. Huckle. Thank you for a most valuable discovery."

"I'll be on my way then. Watch yourself, eh Doctor? You too, Miss Smith."

Huckle left. The Doctor turned to Corporal

Palmer, who was rubbing his eyes and staring dazedly at the message slip still clutched in his hand. "All right, old chap?" asked the Doctor kindly.

"Just about, thanks," said Palmer.

The Brigadier, who had been last to collapse, was the last to wake up. He was somewhat taken aback to find himself stretched out on the floor. A little sheepishly, he got to his feet. "Ah, there you are Doctor. Er—what was I doing down there?"

"Just having a little nap, Brigadier."

The Brigadier glared at him sternly. "Me? Asleep? On duty? There are times, Doctor, when you talk the most absolute rubbish!"

The Doctor grinned at Sarah, and returned to studying the device.

Out on Tulloch Moor, Benton was looking grimly at the broken body of the dead soldier, wondering what colossal weight could have flattened a man like that. Benton had checked up on his network of patrols, and found most of them gradually coming to, with no real idea of what had happened. Those nearest the village had been affected most deeply. Some of that lot were *still* asleep. Eventually, all the men had been accounted for except one, the solitary sentry on the far edge of the patrol area. Benton had rounded up a few of the recovered men and started a search. It hadn't been easy to find the missing man. His body had been half-buried, stamped deep into the ground.

One of the soldiers said, "Shall I order up a stretcher party, sir?"

"Not yet. Nobody's to touch him till the Doctor's had a look!" Benton reached for his RT set.

As soon as they got Benton's message, the Doctor and the Brigadier prepared to leave. The Doctor could see Sarah wasn't really keen on the trip, and after all her recent ordeals he didn't blame her. "Why don't you stay here and guard the fort," he suggested, locking the device away in a drawer. "No need for you to come out in the cold."

Sarah agreed gratefully, and the Doctor and the Brigadier rushed out. She sat down a bit shakily, suddenly hit by reaction. Corporal Palmer gave her a sympathetic look. "Suppose I see if I can rustle up some tea, miss?"

"That'd be marvelous. You'll find the whole place in chaos, I imagine. They'll all be waking up and wondering what hit them."

"Don't worry, miss. Make it myself if I have to," said Palmer, and went off to the kitchens.

On his spyscreen, Broton smiled in satisfaction. "Excellent! Now the human female is alone."

The Doctor and his party drove swiftly to the coordinates Benton had given them, and found him waiting by the body of the dead soldier. The Doctor examined the body. The Brigadier looked on, his face bleak and angry. "Why, Doctor?" he demanded angrily. "Why did they have to murder one of my men?"

The Doctor straightened up. "I know how you feel, Brigadier. It's small consolation, but I don't think it was exactly murder. More a kind of tragic accident. He got in the thing's way and it simply—ran over him."

The Brigadier nodded to Benton, and a stretcher party began carrying the body away. Thankful for the distraction Benton said, "There's something else, sir. I ordered a quick search of the area. They found some . . . traces."

He led them a short distance across the moor, to a patch of boggy ground, where the tough grass of the moor was replaced by squelching mud. Benton pointed. Stretching across the soft ground was a line of enormous claw tracks.

Sarah, meanwhile, alone in UNIT HQ, was amazed and delighted to see Harry Sullivan walk through the door. She jumped up and ran to him, questions pouring out of her. "Harry! How marvelous! Are you all right? What happened to you?"

Harry stepped aside and slipped past her, his voice cold and formal. "Nothing happened. I escaped." He looked round the room. "Where is the trilanic activator?"

"The how much?"

"The device Huckle gave to the Doctor. Where is it?"

"Over there. The Doctor locked it in the drawer."

Harry Sullivan walked over to the drawer,

tried it, then simply ripped it open with one savage tug, splintering the wood around the lock.

"Harry, what on earth are you doing? Why do you want that thing?"

"The Doctor asked me to collect it for him."

"Then why didn't *he* tell you where it was? Why didn't he give you the key?"

"It is not important," answered the flat voice.

Suddenly Sarah noticed—there was no bandage round Harry's head—*and no trace of any wound.* She said firmly, "Just you wait a minute, Harry . . ." and stood in the doorway, barring his exit. With a powerful shove, he thrust her to one side and strode out of the room.

This convinced Sarah that she wasn't dealing with the Harry Sullivan she knew. *Her* Harry was the soul of old-fashioned chivalry. He could never bring himself to raise his voice to a lady, let alone his hand. She ran out of the inn and started to chase the intruder down the street.

He was some way ahead by now, marching incredibly quickly with a stiff, robot-like stride. Sarah ran after him calling, "Hey, you—come back!" At the sound of her voice, he quickened his pace. Sarah saw two UNIT soldiers coming down the street just ahead of them. She yelled, "Stop him—he's stolen something of the Doctor's!"

The two soldiers were naturally pretty baffled. They made a half-hearted attempt to stop Harry, who knocked them out of his way and

61

broke into a run. He pelted down a side-street, Sarah and the two soldiers still after him.

He led them through the back streets of the little village at an amazing pace. Sarah and the soldiers soon lost sight of him. They split up, trying to cover all possible escape routes. Tulloch was a small village, and there weren't many places to go.

Almost out of breath now, Sarah found herself outside a barn on the edge of the village. There was no sign of Harry. In fact there was no sign of anyone. Still, the barn *was* a possible hiding place, and Sarah decided to take a look.

She crept cautiously into the shadowed gloom of the interior, squinting a little to adjust her eyes to the darkness. She could make out bales of hay, and some kind of agricultural machinery rusting away in the corner. There was a ladder which led up through a trap-door, obviously to a loft. She took a quick look around the barn and was relieved to find it empty. Then she started to climb the ladder. She was half-way up when she thought she heard a sound. She paused. "Harry—Harry, is that you?"

There was no reply, and Sarah climbed the rest of the way. She found herself in a big shadowy loft, half-filled with more bales of hay.

Suddenly, terrifyingly, Harry charged at her from behind one of the stacks. He held a pitchfork before him like a spear, the sharp spikes aimed at her heart. Sarah screamed, turned to run, tripped and fell. Her attacker, unable to arrest his wild charge, tripped over her body and pitched headfirst through the trap door.

Sarah got to her hands and knees, crawled to the edge of the trap-door, and looked down. Spread-eagled on the floor of the barn was the body of a Zygon, the shaft of the pitchfork projecting from its chest. The Zygon jerked spasmodically, then lay still.

Harry Sullivan, the *real* Harry Sullivan, was still a helpless prisoner in his alcove on the Zygon ship. As his replica died, Harry screamed, straining frantically against his bonds. Then he fell back unconscious.

In the Zygon control room, Broton frowned at a wildly flickering gauge. "The Response Monitor on the latest human captive indicates an autonomous reflex."

A Zygon came to look at the dial. Respectfully it said, "That is impossible, Commander. Unless . . ."

"Unless something has happened to Madra. Check the synchron response."

Obediently the Zygon examined its console. "There *is* no synchron response, Commander."

"Then Madra has been eliminated." Broton's voice rose to an angry screech. "Immediate molecular dispersal. The humans must not find his body. Immediate dispersal."

The Zygon touched more control nodules and there was a sudden hum of power.

Sarah climbed slowly down the ladder, and

63

stood looking at the dead Zygon. She heard the clattering of boots outside and yelled, "This way. It's in here! Hurry!"

The dead Zygon at her feet began to glow with a fierce light. It blurred, shimmered and faded to nothingness. The pitchfork, with nothing to support it, clattered to the floor of the barn. Beside it lay the alien signal device.

UNIT soldiers rushed into the barn, rifles at the ready. They found Sarah staring at an empty patch of floor.

"Er—*what's* in here, Miss?" asked one of them politely.

Sarah looked at him. "But it was *there*—" she protested.

The soldiers looked at her blankly. Sarah sighed. "Come on," she said. "We'd better get this back to HQ." She picked up the signaling device, and led the way out of the barn.

Back at the inn she told her story to the Doctor and the Brigadier, who had just returned from their trip to the moor. The Brigadier looked as baffled as his soldiers, but the Doctor listened with absorbed attention. "Molecular rearrangement, too," he said thoughtfully. "We're dealing with a very advanced species. Still, thanks to you, Sarah, we've at least got their signaling device. And there's something else. If they can make a replica of Harry, there's a good chance the original's still alive!"

"What worries me," said Sarah pensively, "is—how did they know we had that thing?"

The Doctor looked at her. "That's a very good point, Sarah. They knew exactly where to come for it, didn't they?"

Hesitantly Sarah said, "It probably sounds silly—but I keep getting a feeling we're being watched."

The Doctor rubbed his chin, and turned to the Brigadier. "They do seem to know our moves in advance, don't they?"

The Brigadier was outraged. "You mean they're spying on us?"

"Some form of electronic surveillance, perhaps. We know their technology is of a very high order."

"A bug, you mean?" The Brigadier pronounced the slang term with distaste.

"Precisely, Brigadier. A bug!"

Relieved to have a problem he knew how to deal with, the Brigadier snapped, "Mr. Benton, I want every part of this building checked for bugs, understand?"

In the Zygon control room, Broton switched off his spy screen with an angry hiss. "This Doctor and his friends must be destroyed. *Totally* destroyed. Program the Skarasen to attack."

His second-in-command hissed in alarm. "Is that wise, Commander? You have always said that we must conceal our presence on this planet until—"

Broton was too angry to listen. "I will not tolerate argument from my subordinates," he screamed. "The Doctor suspects too much of the truth. He must be crushed before he can prove his theories and mobilize the planet against us. Prepare the attack program!"

The Doctor would have been flattered to know that the Zygons considered him such a menace. With the aid of some hastily rigged-up scanning equipment, he was studying the signal device and making very little progress. The Brigadier and Sarah looked on sympathetically, understanding his rage and frustration, but unable to help.

The Doctor threw down the device and looked up. "Not metallic, certainly. It *must* be a carbon structure. It's either that, or vareldemyte in organic suspension—don't you agree?"

"I'm sure you're right, Doctor," said Sarah soothingly.

The Doctor grinned in spite of himself. "Well, I wish I was."

Sarah stared at the device as it lay on the table. She gave a sudden squeak. "It moved, Doctor! I saw it move."

They all looked at the device. It moved again, edging slowly across the table, as if trying to escape.

The Doctor blocked its path with a telephone directory. "Just as I thought. Part artifact, part organic!"

As though frustrated by its imprisonment, the

device began giving out a high-pitched electronic burbling sound.

Cautiously, the Brigadier said, "What's it *doing*, Doctor?"

"Signaling!" announced the Doctor, with evident satisfaction.

Sarah looked at him nervously. "Does that mean the creature that smashed the rigs could be on its way here?"

"That's right," answered the Doctor happily. He seemed to be rather pleased at the idea.

"I see," said the Brigadier crisply. "Well, we'd better prepare for it. I'll get the machine guns issued."

The Doctor shook his head. "Might as well hunt elephants with a pea-shooter."

"Then what *do* we do?"

The Doctor picked up the device. "Only one thing for it. I'll try to draw it off. I'll take the calling devide out onto Tulloch Moor." He nodded toward the tracking equipment in the corner. "Meanwhile, your chaps can use my equipment to try and trace the activating signal. If your men on Point McNab are on their toes, we'll be able to get a proper fix on these aliens and find their base."

The Brigadier assessed the plan and agreed. It was their only chance. "Very well, Doctor. Corporal Palmer!" Palmer was already at the Doctor's tracking device, gently adjusting the controls, as the Doctor made for the door.

Sarah said, "*Must* you, Doctor? It's an awful

risk. You don't know how fast that thing can move."

The Doctor chuckled. "Don't worry, Sarah. It doesn't know how fast I can move. Besides, if we're going to rescue poor Harry, we *must* find that base."

The Doctor drove his borrowed landrover out of the village, and headed for Tulloch Moor. His plan was very simple. He would make the monster chase him for as long as he could, to give the Brigadier and his men the best possible chance of tracing the transmitting signal. If the creature got too close, he'd simply have to throw away the calling device and run for it. The monster would probably be satisfied once it found the device. And even if it did come after him, the Doctor wasn't too worried. He didn't have a very high opinion of monsters, however large and powerful. The bigger, the stupider, in his experience. With the whole of Tulloch Moor to play around in he was confident he could elude the thing almost indefinitely.

The Doctor drove to the center of the moor and waited. For a while nothing happened. Darkness began to gather around him as he sat there, increasing the effect of the mist that drifted over the moor. Suddenly, he heard a roar. Then another and another. They sounded steadily louder as the creature got nearer. The Doctor took the still bleeping calling-device from his pocket. He guessed it was leading the creature straight to him.

He pressed the starter on the landrover. It was here that his plan met with its *first* setback. The engine turned over once, coughed, and died. The Doctor checked the fuel tank. Empty! The landrover had seen a lot of use that day, and there had been just enough fuel left to get the Doctor to the middle of Tulloch Moor.

He climbed out of the landrover, still not too dismayed. Maybe he'd do better on foot, since he'd make a smaller target.

A shattering roar sounded almost in his ear. He looked up and saw the long waving neck of the monster above the trees, the fierce head casting about in search of him. The Doctor had a fleeting impression of its size and power. Then an angry roar reminded him that it was time to get moving.

He ran from the landrover as fast as he could, undeterred by the gathering darkness and the uneven ground. His long legs took him across the moor at a tremendous speed, tartan scarf flying out behind him. But fast as the Doctor was, the monster was even faster. The next roar was so loud that he felt it must be breathing down his neck. Reluctantly the Doctor decided it was already time to abandon the signaling device. And it was here that he suffered his *second* setback. He flung the thing away from him with all his strength, then realized to his horror that it was still in his hand. Worse than that, it was now *fixed*. It had extruded powerful little tentacles which wound tightly round his wrist.

The Doctor tugged at the device frantically, perfectly willing to lose a little skin if it would save his life. But it was no use. He couldn't shift it. He heard another roar even closer, looked up and saw the huge bulk of the monster bearing down on him like an express train. Abandoning any attempt to lose the signaling device, the Doctor ran for his life.

At UNIT HQ the Brigadier was poised over the map. "The second bearing's coming through now, sir," said Palmer. "Bearing Two-o-one."

"Right!" the Brigadier was exultant. "We've got their base. First bearing was One-seven-nine, so that puts the transmitter—*here!*"

He jabbed a finger at the map. Sarah looked over his shoulder.

"Loch Ness!"

"That's right," said the Brigadier. "Loch Ness!"

"Well, we've got the information," said Sarah. "Now all we need is the Doctor." From somewhere on the moor came a series of ferocious roars.

The Doctor was tiring fast now. Already he seemed to have covered most of Tulloch Moor. He dodged and weaved, used every scrap of cover, but the huge creature behind him matched his every move.

Finally, inevitably, the Doctor slipped. His foot turned in a patch of mud, and he crashed to the ground, half-stunned. It took him a moment to recover his breath, and as he started to scramble to his feet, he saw it was too late. The monster was almost upon him.

In the Zygon ship, Harry Sullivan recovered consciousness. To his astonishment he found that the fibers which had held him were now dangling limply. He was free! He stepped from the alcove and began creeping steadily toward the control room.

Broton meanwhile was preparing to enjoy the death of the Doctor from a front-row seat. A special monitor screen, linked to the optical system of the Skarasen, showed him the scene on the moor through the monster's eyes. Broton felt as if he *were* the Skarasen, looking down from his mighty height at the puny figure of the Doctor. "Kill him," hissed Broton. *"Kill him!"*

Through the cold, misty darkness of the moor, the Doctor saw the savage head of the monster lunge toward him. . . .

7

Hunt for a Zygon

Harry Sullivan crept along the tangled corridors of the Zygon spaceship. There was no clear plan in his mind, though he was desperately hoping to find a way out. He still wasn't over the shock of seeing a Zygon replica of himself. The thought that the false Harry Sullivan was somewhere outside, perhaps trying to harm his friends, made him frantic to escape. Failing that, he was determined to sabotage the ship, doing as much damage as he could before they recaptured him.

He reached the entrance to the control room as Broton was crouched over his monitor screen, determined to extract the last bit of enjoyment from the Doctor's death. Over Broton's shoulder Harry could see the Doctor, trying to escape from something that towered high above him.

Instinctively, Harry dashed into the control room and hurled himself at the console nearest the Skarasen screen. Before the astonished Zygons could stop him, he banged, thumped and twisted every control in sight, and finally gave the console a tremendous kick. There was an angry electronic screech as the sensitive Zygon control system was thrown into confusion. Angry Zygons closed in on Harry from all sides, and delivered a series of stinging shocks that dropped him to the floor. But the damage was done. Although Harry did not know it, his impulsive action had saved the Doctor's life.

On the moor, the Skarasen gave a roar of distress as its guidance system was thrown completely out of gear. The long neck lashed about wildly, no longer seeking the Doctor, who took the opportunity to roll clear. At the same time, the tentacles that had clamped the signaling device to the Doctor's wrist went limp. It fell to the ground and the massive foot of the monster crashed down upon it, shattering it to pieces. The Skarasen, roaring wildly, disappeared into the mist.

The Doctor, lying face downward in a patch of mud, realized with some surprise that he was still alive. He looked at his now-empty hand— the gripping tentacles had made weals in the flesh of his wrist. He began searching the immediate area, and with some difficulty collected the smashed fragments of the calling device. Putting them carefully in his pocket, he set off for the inn.

While Harry lay unconscious on the floor of the control room, the frantic Zygons worked to restore normal operation. Broton stood over them, hissing angrily, "Hurry, you fools. Hurry!"

The Zygon Chief Engineer looked up from his console. "The target reciprocator is dead, Commander. We have lost visual contact." The screen that "saw" through the eyes of the monster showed only a confused pattern of disturbance signals.

Broton said thoughtfully, "The target reciprocator was attached to the Doctor. It can be destroyed only by the Skarasen. If the reciprocator is dead—then so it the Doctor!" He inspected the work of the Zygon engineer. Their frantic efforts had nearly completed the repairs. "As soon as you are finished, recall the Skarasen." He kicked at the inert body of Harry. "How did this creature escape?"

"When the replica was killed, the body print mechanism must have fused. Shall we kill him, Commander?"

Broton considered. "No. Not yet. He may still be of use to us. Put him in the cell." The Zygons dragged Harry from the room.

When the Doctor failed to return from the moor, Sarah and the Brigadier set off in a landrover to find him. Warrant Officer Benton stayed behind to supervise the final stages of what the men already called, "the Brigadier's bug hunt." They were checking over the parlor when Angus the landlord came in. He looked indignantly at the soldiers swarming everywhere, peering behind pictures, under carpets, tapping sections of wall, and glancing beneath ashtrays and lamp stands. "Hey—now—what do you think you're doing?"

Benton emerged from underneath the sofa. "Brigadier's orders, Mr. MacRanald. We're looking for bugs."

Angus was outraged. "Bugs, is it? You can tell yon Brigadier that this is a clean house."

"Not that sort of bug," explained Benton patiently. "Microphones. Spying equipment."

"Och, you're all mad. Who'd be hiding microphones in here?"

"Better ask the Brigadier."

Angus rounded on one of the searching soldiers. "Just mind what you're doing with that bedwarmer. It was said to belong to the Duke of Cumberland."

"All right, we believe you!" Benton took the heavy copper warming pan from the soldier, looked it over, and hung it carefully back on the wall. "O.K., Jackson, check the window area."

Angus shook his head in disgust. "You're wasting your time. In Tulloch we don't need any clever contraptions to know what folks are up to. Everybody knows everybody's business as a matter of principle."

Benton turned his attention to the stag's head on the wall. As he reached up, Angus called, "And keep your clumsy hands off that. It was a gift, from the Duke of Forgill himself."

"Keep your hair on," said Benton soothingly.

Since the Brigadier had told him to do his best to avoid upsetting Angus, he gave the stag's head no more than a cursory examination before carrying on with the search.

In the Zygon control room, Broton switched off the spy screen. "They are becoming suspicious. Tomorrow that monitor link must be removed."

It was almost dark now, and it was no easy task to find the Doctor in the gloom of the misty moor. The Brigadier, methodical as ever, searched section by section. Sarah checked the map beside him. She looked up impatiently as yet another area proved blank. "Can't we hurry it up, Brigadier?"

The Brigadier studied his compass. "If we dash about all over the place, we're certain to lose him. System and method, Miss Smith. It's the only way."

Eventually the Brigadier's patience was rewarded. They found the Doctor's abandoned landrover. The Brigadier made a note of its position so that he could send a recovery team. A search of the surrounding area led them to the place where the Skarasen had almost pinned the Doctor down. Sarah shuddered as she looked at the churned-up ground. "Something happened here all right—but what?"

The Brigadier jumped from the landrover and made a careful examination of the ground.

"Well, since there's no sign of a body, or of any blood, we can assume the Doctor managed to survive. Now, once he escaped the monster, what would be his next move?"

"He'd go home?" suggested Sarah.

"Precisely!" The Brigadier jumped back behind the wheel. "And since we know the Doctor has an excellent sense of direction, we'll find him somewhere on the direct route between here and the inn."

Sure enough the headlights of the landrover picked up the Doctor's tall form about ten minutes later. He was trudging rather wearily toward home. Even for the Doctor, it had been a long, hard day.

The Brigadier pulled up beside him. The Doctor climbed into the landrover and settled into the back seat with a grateful sigh.

"Are you all right, Doctor?" Sarah asked anxiously. "What happened?"

The Doctor told them of his narrow escape. "Luckily for me, the cyborg overstepped its mark," he concluded. He did not know yet about Harry's handy intervention.

"Cyborg, eh?" said the Brigadier. "You were right about the creature then?"

"Oh, I think so. Somebody was controlling it, with the help of this." The Doctor showed them the shattered remains of the calling device.

"What exactly *is* a cyborg?" asked Sarah.

"A sort of hybrid creation, half animal, half

machine. Oh, they must be a *very* interesting species."

"Who must?" demanded the Brigadier.

"Whoever's controlling this monster. Fascinating technology! Now then, was my little romp all in vain, or did you manage to locate their base?"

Sarah produced a map. "There, you see, Doctor? Under Loch Ness, fairly close to the shore."

The Doctor frowned. "And very close to Forgill Castle."

They could see the lights of the village ahead of them now.

The Brigadier said over his shoulder, "Well, Doctor, what's your next move?"

The Doctor yawned and stretched. "A hot bath, I think. Then a very large meal, and a nice long sleep."

"That isn't *exactly* what I meant . . ."

"And in the morning," the Doctor went on, "I think we'll pay a visit to Forgill Castle."

Angus MacRanald was up early next morning, checking that everything was running smoothly. He'd already served breakfast to three of his guests. Now he looked disgustedly around his best parlor, which was filled with trestle tables, filing cabinets, RT equipment and all the paraphernalia of UNIT's temporary HQ. Still, he had to admit they paid well. And they did seem to be taking reasonable care of the place.

Angus began emptying ashtrays, and generally tidying up. Proudly he reached up and dusted the heavy wooden plaque on which the stag's head was mounted. A fine man, the Duke, even if he had been a wee bit strange of late. It took a real aristocrat to be so generous—the stag's head was a splendid gift. Angus ran his duster lightly over the stag's face, flicking dust from the creature's prominently bulging eyes. Then he blinked. Had he imagined it—or had one of the eyes moved? Maybe it was loose—he didn't want it falling out.

Standing on a chair, Angus peered more closely at the glassy eye. It seemed to swivel. He prodded it gently and it dropped into his hand. The socket of the eye was filled with miniaturized electronic equipment. Angus was so intent on his discovery that he didn't notice the door of the room opening. He heard a voice behind him. "And what are you doing up there, Mr. MacRanald?"

Angus looked down. It was Sister Lamont, the nurse from the oil company's sick bay. He was too wrapped-up in his discovery to wonder why she was at the inn so early. "The soldier laddies reckoned they were being bugged," he said excitedly. "Sure enough, I think I've found it. Though how anybody could have fixed . . ."

Angus's voice tailed away. He rubbed a hand over his eyes, and got down from the chair.

Something seemed to be happening to Sister Lamont. She was shimmering, blurring somehow. She was changing her shape. As the Zygon advanced toward him, claw-like hand outstretched, Angus MacRanald backed away and screamed. . . .

Benton was crossing the yard of the inn when he heard the appalling sound. He ran toward the parlor at once, calling to a couple of his men to follow.

They clattered into the room and halted. Angus lay sprawled on the floor under the stag's head. Benton checked his pulse, but Angus was quite dead, his heart stopped by the massive blast of the Zygon sting. The window was open wide.

Benton snapped, "Get your rifles and follow me. We'll search the area. It can't have gone far . . ."

Benton was right. Disturbed by the immediate arrival of the soldiers, the Zygon had not had time to reassume human shape. It had been forced to leave the form of Sister Lamont in order to attack Angus—a Zygon can use its power to "sting" only when in its proper form. Now it was scuttling through the fields that bordered the inn, heading for the nearby woods. It hoped to find some hiding place in which to reassume the shape of Sister Lamont and then return innocently to the sick bay. Although it was easy enough to revert to Zygon form, taking the shape of a human required considerable effort, and the alien needed at least a few minutes of peace and quiet to achieve the necessary concentration.

Unfortunately for the Zygon, it was spotted almost immediately. One of the soldiers saw the crouched-over, orange-green shape scuttling into the woods. He fired: the creature staggered, but ran on. "There it goes!" he yelled. Like a fox detected by hounds, the Zygon ran frantically through the woods, a squad of excited UNIT soldiers hallooing behind. The hunt was on!

8

A Visit to the Duke

Even earlier that same morning, the Doctor too had risen, making sure the Brigadier and Sarah were awake with hearty shouts and loud bangs on the doors of their respective rooms. Sarah groaned as she struggled into her clothes. She should have realized that, in the Doctor's terms, a nice long sleep meant something like three or four hours. Indeed, it was something of a novelty for the Doctor to bother with sleep at all.

They made a hasty breakfast of Angus's porridge. Sarah and the Brigadier scandalized him by demanding milk and sugar. The Doctor, in true Highland fashion, ate his with just a sprinkle of salt, saying something about having acquired a taste for it during the Jacobite rebellion.

Now, at a time that Sarah called crack of dawn, and even the Brigadier considered an ungodly hour, the Doctor, wide awake and appallingly cheerful, was driving them up to the doors of Forgill Castle.

Even in the bright morning sunlight, Forgill Castle looked like that place in Transylvania where Frankenstein carried out his dreadful experiments, and Count Dracula flitted around the battlements at sunset. Sarah was glad they'd come in the morning. She'd have hated to visit the place after dark.

The Doctor whizzed the landrover across the drawbridge and pulled up in a flagged courtyard in front of the main entrance. He jumped out and, without bothering to knock, pushed the heavy door, which creaked open. The Doctor stepped inside, followed rather more hesitantly by Sarah and the Brigadier.

They found themselves in an imposing baronial hall, stone-flagged, furnished with massive tables and chairs. The far wall was entirely covered by bookshelves, and a huge oak table was piled with dusty papers. The traditional suits of armor stood about like sinister guardians, and a great stone staircase led up into shadowy darkness. The whole place was deserted. Sarah and the Brigadier looked around in respectful silence.

The Doctor, who sometimes seemed to have no proper feelings, made them jump by suddenly bellowing, "Shop!" His voice echoed hollowly round the great stone room.

The Brigadier shot him a reproachful glance and called out, "Your Grace? Is anyone there?"

Silence. Sarah looked worried. "I really don't think we should have come in unannounced."

"Nobody around to announce us, was there?" said the Doctor unrepentantly. "Apparently most of the staff have gone off to work for the oil company. Can't say I blame them, either."

The Doctor flung himself into one of the high-backed chairs, and managed to produce quite a credible imitation of the Duke's voice. "My family has served this country for seven centuries," he said haughtily. "That seems not to count, these days!"

He looked expectantly at the Brigadier and Sarah, waiting for applause. But no one was laughing. The Doctor turned. The Duke of Forgill was descending the staircase toward them.

At the bottom of the steps the Duke paused and said coldly, "Perhaps you would explain this intrusion? I'm afraid the Castle is not open to the public."

The Doctor was quite unabashed. "Nobody answered the front door, so we just barged in."

"You have some reason for calling?"

"Oh, yes," answered the Doctor cheerfully.

"Well?"

"My friend the Brigadier will explain."

Hastily the Brigadier said, "Ah, yes well, the fact is . . ." His voice tailed off.

"The fact is *what*?"

By now the Doctor was wandering around the hall peering at the shields and weapons which hung from the walls. Realizing that he wasn't going to be any help, the Brigadier began again. "Well, sir, we have reason to believe there is something peculiar in Loch Ness, quite close to this castle."

The Duke's voice was scornful. "You don't mean to tell me you've found the monster?"

Sarah said defiantly, "As it happens, your Grace, that's exactly what we do mean."

"I do believe you're serious!"

The Doctor raised the visor on a suit of armor and let it down with a clang. "Oh we are," he said. "Very!"

Pulling himself together, the Brigadier gave the Duke a potted history of recent events. He ended with their discovery that the alien base was somewhere underwater in Loch Ness, just offshore, and fairly close to the castle.

He stumbled to the end of his explanation, not helped by the expression of disbelief plainly visible on the Duke's face. "I see. And what do you intend to do about the aliens, Brigadier?"

Here the Brigadier was on firmer ground. Direct military action was always his forte. "I'm having some depth charges flown up right away—they'll be here this morning. . . . With your Grace's permission, since our target is so close to the castle, I propose to use them at once."

"Depth charges?" the Duke sounded horrified. "You can't explode depth charges in Loch Ness."

"It's the only answer, your Grace. These creatures have given every proof that they're hostile. They, and the monster they control, must be destroyed."

The Doctor had drifted back toward them,

and the Duke turned to him in appeal. "And you, Doctor? Are you a party to this militaristic nonsense?"

The Doctor smiled. "The Brigadier does have a rather touching faith in high explosive as a universal solution," he admitted. "And at the moment, I simply can't think of an alternative."

Sarah looked at the Doctor curiously. It was very unlike him to go along so tamely with the Brigadier. He usually had some quite different, and of course far superior, plan of his own, since he was very much opposed to dealing with problems by blowing them up. She had often heard him expressing his scorn for the limitations of the military mind. Why was he being amenable? Sarah had a feeling that something was going on under the surface of the conversation between the Doctor and the Duke. It was as if they were fighting a kind of verbal duel.

The Duke paused for a moment. He spoke slowly and carefully, marshaling his arguments. "There is no proof—there never has been any proof—that the monster exists."

"It exists all right," said Sarah indignantly. "Last night it chased the Doctor halfway across Tulloch Moor."

"What's more," added the Brigadier, "we believe it has been attacking the oil rigs."

"Loch Ness is seven miles from the coast. Are you suggesting the monster can cross that distance to the sea without being seen?"

"Maybe there's an underground river," suggested Sarah.

"Hardly. Loch Ness is too high above sea level."

"But there *is* an underground channel, your Grace." The Doctor spoke with calm assurance. "It runs from Loch Ness to the Devil's Punchbowl, the small Loch near the village, and close to the sea. That's the monster's back door."

"I've never heard such nonsense. Are you seriously suggesting the monster commutes between here and the North Sea whenever it feels like it?"

"Whenever it's ordered to," corrected the Doctor. "It obeys some kind of control system."

"Whose control system?"

"The aliens."

"*What* aliens?"

"I know how you feel, your Grace," said the Brigadier sympathetically. "Before I joined UNIT, I was pretty sceptical about such things myself."

"You're mad, all of you," exploded the Duke." Aliens working monsters by remote control!"

Sarah felt the Doctor wasn't taking the Duke seriously. He was studying him, rather like someone watching a clever performance. He beamed amiably at the angry Duke. "Well, it takes all sorts to make a galaxy—doesn't it, your Grace? No doubt the aliens have problems of their own." Once again Sarah sensed a hidden meaning behind the apparently foolish remark.

The Doctor wandered off, this time to look at the rows of bookshelves lining the far wall. The Duke followed him. "As you can see, most of these books are devoted to the subject of the monster. Sightings have been reported ever since the Middle Ages. Your aliens must have lived under the loch for many centuries."

"Perhaps they have, your Grace. Many species have life spans far longer than that of human beings."

"Then why should they suddenly become aggressive?"

Sarah said, "Surely it must be something to do with the oil?"

The Doctor nodded. "That could be part of the answer. For hundreds of years the monster was able to cross Tulloch Moor, on its way to the North Sea to feed. Then the oil company built their base right across its path. It was forced to detour, passing close to the village. That, Brigadier, is why its masters released nerve gas—and why you and your men went to sleep."

"Are you suggesting the thing's attacking oil rigs just because it had to go out of its way a bit?"

"There must be more to it than that. I think its masters have recently changed their plans— some new development we don't know about yet. It's a pity they reacted with unintelligent violence—don't you agree, your Grace?"

The ringing of the telephone sounded strangely out of place in the castle hall. The Duke crossed to an old-fashioned instrument fastened to a pillar and answered it. "Yes? Yes, he's here." He beckoned to the Brigadier, who took the receiver with a nod of thanks.

"Yes? They have? Splendid. We'll come at once." Exultantly he slammed down the receiver. "We may be able to convince you about the aliens after all, your Grace. I'm not sure of the details yet, but my men seem to have cornered one on the moor. Coming, Doctor?" The Brigadier was already on his way.

The Doctor reached for his hat. "Sarah?"

Sarah didn't move. "Do you think I might stay here for a while, your Grace? I'd very much like to look through your library. I could do some research for a story on the monster."

The Doctor looked dubious. "I'm really not sure that's wise, Sarah."

"Why not? I might even turn up a valuable lead. And if the Duke doesn't mind . . ."

The Doctor looked questioningly at the Duke, who said, "Why not? I assure you, the young lady will be quite safe."

"Well, at least we'll know where she is," said the Doctor.

Once again Sarah sensed a hidden meaning beneath the exchange. "All right, Sarah. Look out for any references to MacRanald Bay and the Devil's Punchbowl. And stay here, won't you? Don't go wandering about all over the place." With a hasty wave of farewell the Doctor followed the Brigadier out to the landrover. The Duke went to see them off and Sarah was left staring thoughtfully at the rows of books. She took off her coat, chose a book at random and started to read.

After a hair-raising drive across Tulloch Moor, the Doctor and the Brigadier found Benton at the edge of a heather-covered hill ringed with UNIT troops. Benton pointed. "It's somewhere up there, sir. One of the men took a shot at it, thinks he winged it. It can't get away—the hill's completely surrounded. Shall I tell the lads to move in?"

The Brigadier nodded. "All right. I want it captured alive, if possible."

"And tell them to be careful," added the Doctor. "They mustn't get too close."

Benton nodded grimly. "Don't worry, Doctor. We know what it can do."

Rifles at the ready, the troops began to move forward, combing through the heather like beaters at a shoot.

Out of sight, on the other side of the hill, a UNIT Corporal was taking advantage of his isolated position to have a quiet smoke. But he was still on the alert, and he whirled around quickly when he heard a rustling behind him. He relaxed as a neat, plain woman in the uniform of a hospital sister came out of the heather, her hands held behind her. "Sorry, Miss, nobody's allowed to pass."

"I'm from the oil company sick-bay. I was told someone was hurt."

"You'd better see Mr. Benton. I'll call him up." He reached for his RT and then paused. There was a small, spreading patch of blood on the Sister's arm. "Hey, you're hurt yourself."

The Sister's hands came from behind her back. In one of them was gripped a jagged chunk of rock. Before the sentry could react she swung it viciously to the side of his head. As he collapsed in the heather, the Zygon jumped into the UNIT landrover and drove off at high speed.

9

The Secret of Forgill Castle

The Brigadier looked down sadly at the body of
Angus MacRanald, then pulled the blanket
back over the dead man's face. He nodded to
the two UNIT soldiers, who picked up the
stretcher and carried it away. The Brigadier felt
responsible for Angus's death. "If we hadn't
commandeered this inn as our HQ . . ."

The Doctor nodded, his face equally grave.
"I know, old chap," he said. "It wasn't your
fault."

Benton came into the room. "I've just been
talking to our chap who got slugged, sir; he recovered consciousness for a few minutes. He
says it was Sister Lamont, from the sick bay.
And one of the lads saw her driving off."

"She was there when Sarah and I got locked
in the decompression chamber," the Doctor
said. They really ought to have done something
about Sister Lamont. Somehow she'd been
overlooked in the rush of events.

"What was she doing *here*?" demanded the
Brigadier. "Why kill poor old Angus?"

"I think Angus was bug-hunting," said the

93

Doctor sadly. "Sister Lamont is one of the aliens. We know from Sarah they can take on human shape. She came to recover the bug and caught him. Look!" He pointed to the stag's head. With a shock the Brigadier saw that the creature's eyes were gone. Its blind stare made the head more sinister than ever. "The Duke of Forgill gave Angus that head," the Doctor continued. "Sarah said he was very proud of it."

"Are you suggesting that his Grace is involved in all this?" The Brigadier's conservative temperament boggled at the idea that a member of the aristocracy could be mixed up in shady doings.

"Of course he's involved," said the Doctor impatiently. "I suspected as much at the castle. The death of poor Angus clinches it."

"Great Scott—the Duke," muttered the Brigadier. "And we left Miss Smith at the castle. We've got to get her back. Come on!"

The Doctor's face was worried as he followed out to the landrover. As Sarah had guessed, he had suspected the Duke from the very first. By revealing how much he knew of their plans, by letting them see how determined the Brigadier was to attack them, the Doctor had hoped to bluff the aliens into seeking a peaceful solution. He'd even agreed to let Sarah stay at the Castle, feeling that he and the Duke had reached a sort of unspoken truce. Now, after seeing the struck-down UNIT soldier and the murdered Angus, the Doctor was having second thoughts. Perhaps the aliens were more savagely hostile than he had realized. Perhaps, by being too clever, he had endangered Sarah's life. As the landrover sped up the road to the castle, the Doctor hoped desperately that Sarah had stayed in the hall where they'd left her. If she went wandering off on her own . . . the Doctor shuddered, remembering Angus's dead face.

The Duke of Forgill looked on with polite interest as Sarah plowed her way through the musty books. She closed the volume she was reading, and pointed to the top shelf. "What are those big books up there?"

"Monastic records, Miss Smith. There was a monastery on this spot in the eleventh century."

"May I have a look?"

"Certainly." The Duke tugged on an old-fashioned bell rope and one of the biggest men Sarah had ever seen came marching into the hall. He bowed and then glanced up questioningly.

"Ah, Caber! Our young guest is about to delve into the mysteries of the past. Fetch her the steps, would you?"

"Very good, your Grace." With a distinctly hostile stare at Sarah the big man marched out again.

Sarah had a nervous impulse to make conversation. "Caber?" she said brightly. "That's an unusual name, surely."

"It's really a kind of nickname," explained the Duke. "He was a champion at tossing the caber—the Highland Games, you know."

The big man returned with a heavy, old-fashioned set of library steps, apparently made from solid oak. He dumped them down next to Sarah, bowed, and stood waiting for instructions. The Duke turned to Sarah. "If you'll excuse me, I have work to do." The Duke and his giant servant left the hall.

Left on her own, Sarah climbed the steps and started examining the books on the top shelf. She found them hard going, especially as several appeared to be written in medieval Latin. She had just decided to abandon the top shelf when her foot slipped, and she nearly fell from the steps. She clutched desperately for a hold on one of the shelves; her flailing foot kicked a book somewhere on the middle row. There was a low hum of power, and below her a section of bookshelf swung away to reveal a secret door. Recovering her balance, Sarah climbed down the steps and peered through the opening. There was nothing but blackness. She hunted around the library and to her delight found a big torch on one of the side tables. She shone it through the opening. A long, low, winding tunnel stretched away before her.

For a moment Sarah wrestled with her conscience, but it didn't put up much of a fight. True, she'd promised the Doctor not to go wandering around the castle, but when a clue like this turned up, it would be a crime not to investigate. Somewhere at the back of her mind was a hope that she might find and rescue Harry Sullivan. Shining the torch before her, she crept cautiously into the tunnel.

It soon became apparent that it was leading downward. It led her on and on, down and down, until Sarah began to wonder where the other end would be. Back in London perhaps, or at least in the cellars of the Tulloch Village Inn. Just when she began to feel she was condemned to wander in the depths of the earth for ever, she felt a faint vibration and a hum of power. A dim glow appeared in the distance. The glow became brighter and soon she didn't need the torch. She turned a corner; the light came from a kind of crystal door stretched across the passage.

She moved closer to the door. To her astonishment, it began to rise silently into the roof. Alarmed, Sarah jumped back; the door came down again. Sarah moved forward, the door went up, and she passed underneath it. Immediately the door came down again, and Sarah, feeling trapped, started to run back. Obligingly the door rose to let her through. Reassured, she went on with her journey.

She was now in a very different kind of corridor. The walls were made of a strange, fibrous material that seemed somehow alive. They glowed with their own inner light, and it felt like moving down a giant, plastic drain pipe.

Although Sarah didn't realize it, she was passing through the airlock tube that connected the access tunnel to the Zygon spaceship laying hidden under the bottom of Loch Ness.

She came to another crystal door and went through. More glowing tunnels, twisting and turning, and then an open area. She saw a row of alcoves, like upright coffins. In each one stood a motionless human figure, its head partially concealed by a transparent dome. Sarah took a closer look. She saw the Duke of Forgill, his servant the Caber, and Sister Lamont from the sick-bay. She soon guessed that these were the *real* humans, kept as models for the aliens to copy. Which meant that Harry Sullivan should be here somewhere. . . .

Sarah moved on, and came to another door. There was a transparent panel in it, and Sarah peered through. To her delight, she saw Harry Sullivan looking back at her.

Harry had been in the Zygon cell for what seemed an eternity, bored out of his mind, but otherwise unharmed. Once the after effects of the Zygon stings had worn off he had felt well enough. The Zygons had even brought him food and water from time to time, though they refused to answer his questions. Harry guessed that either they planned to duplicate him again, or were saving him for interrogation when they were a trifle less busy.

Seeing Sarah filled him with a mixture of relief and alarm. He was overjoyed to be rescued, but he wanted to get them both out of there before Sarah was made prisoner too. "Panel just outside the door," he called. "Press your hand on it." He had observed the way the door worked whenever his food arrived.

Obediently Sarah pressed the panel, and the door slid open. Harry jumped out. He tried to hug Sarah but a sudden thought made her jump back nervously. "It *is* you, isn't it?"

"Well, of course it is," said Harry indignantly. Then he remembered. "I say, they made a replica of me. Did you run into it?" Sarah nodded, and Harry thumped her on the back. "Well don't worry, old girl. This is the genuine Sullivan. Now let's get out of here."

Warlord Broton, in his Duke of Forgill form, came back into the library and saw the secret door standing open. He smiled. Just as he'd thought, the girl had come to spy on him. Now she had fallen into his trap.

He heard someone drive into the courtyard, and went to the door. The Caber was helping Sister Lamont out of the UNIT landrover. The wounded Zygon had made a lengthy detour, returning to the castle only when it was quite sure that UNIT had been shaken off. All three Zygons came into the great hall. Broton indicated the open panel. "The human female has gone into the ship. You two go below and alert the crew." The two Zygons went through into the tunnel, blood dripping from the wounded one's shoulder. Broton closed the secret panel behind them.

In the tunnel, Harry and Sarah heard voices and movement. They ducked into an alcove, scarcely daring to breathe. Sarah peeped out for an instant, and saw the Caber and Sister Lamont coming toward them. Or rather, she thought, their replicas. The real humans were still imprisoned under those sinister transparent domes. She heard their voices as they passed within touching distance.

"Soon we shall be able to revert permanently to our normal form," the Caber was saying. Although still in human shape, he spoke in the hissing tone of a Zygon.

Sister Lamont replied in the same alien voice. "Good. How I loathe this abomination of a body."

The two aliens went on their way. Harry and Sarah waited for a moment then continued their journey toward the surface.

For the second time that day, the Doctor and the Brigadier drove into the courtyard of Forgill Castle. The stolen UNIT landrover was still parked in the courtyard. They pushed open the door and entered the hall. Just as before, the place was deserted.

The Doctor saw Sarah's jacket, thrown over a chair.

"Something's happened to her."

The Brigadier noticed a dark patch on the

floor by the bookshelves. He bent down and touched it. "Blood!"

There was a low hum of power and a section of the bookshelves swung open to reveal Harry and Sarah. Overjoyed at the sight of the Doctor and the Brigadier, Sarah said excitedly, "We've found the alien base. It's under the Loch, just as you thought. And that Duke we met is an imposter . . ."

"What about you two?" asked the Doctor gently.

Sarah looked at him indignantly, then remembered how she'd felt on first seeing Harry. The Doctor laughed. He put an arm around both their shoulders. "It's all right, I can *feel* you're genuine." And indeed he could. There was something odd about all the Zygon replicas, a flatness, a lack of human warmth. "Good to see you again, Harry," he said, shaking him warmly by the hand. "Now then, this tunnel leads to the spaceship, I take it—well done, Sarah."

Eagerly the Doctor stepped into the passage, and vanished into the darkness. Alarmed, Sarah called out, "Doctor, be careful . . ." There was a moment's silence, the sound of a scuffle, then from the blackness of the passage came a fierce shout of rage and pain, in what was unmistakably the Doctor's voice. The Brigadier drew his revolver and made for the passage. Two alien figures appeared, barring his way. He stopped in sheer amazement, never having seen Zygons in their natural shape before.

101

Keeping the creatures covered he spoke over his shoulder to Sarah and Harry. "What the devil are they?"

"They call themselves Zygons," said Harry.

The Brigadier raised his revolver. "Stand aside or I fire."

A voice came from behind him. "If you do, the Doctor dies instantly."

All three turned. Broton, also in his Zygon form, was coming down the staircase. "The Doctor has fallen into my ambush," he said in a gloating voice. "We are leaving in our spaceship, and taking him with us."

"Leaving for where?" demanded Harry. "You said you could never return to your own planet."

"That is so," hissed Broton. "Instead, we shall become the masters of yours."

"Indeed," said the Brigadier coolly. "How do you propose to do that? It'll take more than a few wrecked oil rigs to conquer the Earth."

"Destroying the oil rigs was only the beginning. A small trial of strength for the Skarasen. Our real attack is still to come."

Snatching a leather document case from the table, Broton crossed to the entrance of the secret passage and stepped inside. "Remember, any attempt to follow and the Doctor dies!" He disappeared into the blackness and the door closed behind him.

Sarah and Harry looked at each other in baffled despair. The Brigadier grabbed his walkie-talkie. "Don't worry, we're not beaten yet." Within a few moments he was in contact with HQ. "Benton, are those depth charges here? Excellent! I want them at Forgill Castle—and now!"

Not much later, Harry and Sarah were looking on anxiously as Benton supervised the setting up of a depth charge launcher on the edge of Loch Ness.

"I knew those charges would come in handy," said the Brigadier with evident satisfaction.

"What about the Doctor?" Sarah asked anxiously. "He's down there too, you know."

The Brigadier sighed. "I'm not attempting to *destroy* the ship. I've set the charges to explode high, just to shake 'em up a bit. When they realize we've got 'em cold, they'll come to the surface and surrender. Ready, Mr. Benton?"

Benton nodded. "Ready, sir!"

"Right. Fire one!"

The depth charge flew through the air and disappeared beneath the surface of the loch. Seconds later they heard the rumble of an under-water explosion.

"Fire two!" A second depth-charge, a second explosion.

Deep beneath the waters of the loch, the Zygon ship rocked and shuddered. The Doctor, a prisoner in the control room between two Zygon guards, said affably, "Feels like my old friend the Brigadier. He does love a nice big noise, you know."

"We are attacked," hissed Broton. "Prepare for flight."

Zygon hands moved over control nodules and the hum of power rose to a crescendo.

From the edge of the loch the Brigadier yelled happily, "Give 'em another one!" Another depth-charge flew through the air to splash into the waters of the loch.

The Zygon control room juddered again.

"Report," ordered Broton.

"All damage minor. Main systems functional."

"Maximum flight range?"

"Seven hundred Earth miles."

Another explosion rocked the ship.

On the loch side, the Brigadier gave a smile of satisfaction as the rumble of the last explosion died away. "That should teach 'em we mean business."

In the control room the Doctor looked on with interest as the Zygon crew moved into a final burst of almost panic-stricken activity.

"Activate dynacron thrust," screamed Broton.

The power hum went up another notch, but the Doctor's cheerful voice could still be heard over the din. "Going somewhere, are we?" he asked cheerfully.

The Brigadier and his friends watched the still surface of the loch. Suddenly the water began to steam and bubble. The Brigadier nodded in satisfaction. "You see—they're coming up."

And indeed the Zygons were coming up, but not in the way the Brigadier had imagined, like a World War II submarine surfacing to surrender. Looking like a vast, barnacle-covered crab shell, the Zygon ship broke the surface of the loch like an underwater missile, and shot straight up into the air.

The Brigadier, Sarah and Harry watched as the strangely shaped vessel streaked up into the sky and disappeared over the trees. "Well, Brigadier," said Sarah grimly. "What now?"

For once the Brigadier was lost for words.

10

Plan for Conquest

It took the Brigadier only a moment to recover his self-possession. "Benton! Get the men back into the vehicles. We'll be leaving here right away."

Harry gazed up into the sky trying to catch a last glimpse of the disappearing spaceship. "Where can they be heading? Broton said their ship was crippled."

In the Zygon control room, Broton snapped, "Check remar pulsator."

"You'll never get this old banger out of Earth's gravity," said the Doctor cheerfully. "Your dynacron drive's out of phase—listen!" And indeed there was an irregular jarring note in the electronic hum filling the control room.

"Silence," hissed Broton. "Unnecessary speech is forbidden here."

"No wonder your conversation's so dull . . ." The Doctor knew he'd made a mistake as soon as he spoke. He'd finally driven Broton too far. The Zygon lunged forward, claw-like hand outstretched, and sent a savage blast of energy through the Doctor that dropped him unconscious to the floor.

Beside the loch, the Brigadier was barking orders into his walkie-talkie. "That's right, emergency alert to all radar stations. Alien spacecraft heading due south from Loch Ness.

"Alert Strike Command, but warn them there is to be no attack, I repeat, no attack, until ordered by me. Have my aircraft standing by at Inverness, fueled for immediate return to London. That is all. Out."

The Brigadier jumped into his landrover, where Harry and Sarah were waiting for him.

"Brigadier," asked Sarah, "Shouldn't we search the castle before we leave?"

"What for? There's nobody there now."

"We might find some kind of clue. Something to tell us where the Zygons have gone."

"Or at least what they plan to do," supported Harry.

The Brigadier looked dubious. "Suppose it might be worth a look—just on the off-chance. I've got to get back to Tulloch and co-ordinate things. I'll drop you two off at the castle, if you like."

The Doctor recovered consciousness in the little cell that had once held Harry Sullivan. He heard Broton's voice. "The humans will attempt to follow our course by their primitive radar. Transmit maximum jamming signal."

108

"Yes, Commander." The other Zygon marched away.

Weakly the Doctor said, "You've been hiding too long, Broton. It's become a habit."

Broton looked down at him dispassionately. "What do you mean?"

"I thought your plan was to rule the world?"

"The plan has not changed."

The Doctor struggled to his feet. "Well, there you are then. You can't rule the world if you're in hiding. You have to step out on a balcony from time to time and wave a gracious claw."

It was obvious Broton didn't share the Doctor's sense of humor. "In a few hours," he said solemnly, "there will be no more need for secrecy. Have no doubt, Doctor, your world will recognize its new master."

A wave of giddiness came over the Doctor and he leaned against the cell wall. Two Zygon stings in rapid succession had been a bit much, even for his resilient constitution. "Well, Broton, we shall see what we shall see!" he said feebly. It wasn't much of a riposte, but it was the best he could manage for the moment.

Sarah and Harry spent a long time searching the castle, but they found nothing to give them a clue to Broton's destination. The castle was so huge that it would have taken an army to do a proper job, so they concentrated on the few rooms that showed signs of habitation, particularly the great hall where Broton appeared to have spent most of his time.

Sarah went through a pile of papers on the desk, most of them to do with the management of the Duke's estate, though there were also some connected with an Energy Conference in London. "Harry," she said, "when you were a prisoner didn't Broton tell you anything about his plans?"

"He did a lot of boasting but nothing specific. I got the idea he's planning some great gesture of destruction, something to make the world sit up and notice him."

"Something bigger than smashing up oil rigs?"

"I suppose it must be."

"If only we knew what, there might be some chance of helping the Doctor." Sarah stared around the room, biting her lower lip in concentration.

Harry dusted what felt like the dust of centuries from his hands. "Doesn't look as if we're going to find anything, old girl."

Sarah took a last look around the cluttered room. In the end it was something that wasn't even there, not something that was, that gave them their only clue.

"Document case!" said Sarah suddenly. "You remember, Broton was very careful to take it when he went off." In her mind's eye she could still see the expensive leather case clutched in the alien claw. "Now why would he take the Duke's document case?"

Harry shrugged. "Maybe he fancied a souvenir! Come on, let's get back to HQ. I'll ring Tulloch for some transport."

As Harry went to the telephone, Sarah stood lost in thought. She didn't realize it, but noticing the missing document case was the nearest she'd come yet to discovering the Zygons' plans.

The Zygons' crippled ship flew just above the layer of low cloud. Broton knew they would have to land soon. For all his boastings, the patched-up, crippled ship couldn't last much longer. That was why he had reacted so violently to the Doctor's taunts.

With a surge of relief he heard his engineer say, "We have discovered a possible landing zone, Commander."

Immediately Broton said, "Prepare for descent." Whatever if was, it would have to do.

The chief engineer ordered, "Reduce dynacron thrust."

"Dynacron thrust at phase—"

"Initiate descent trajectory," hissed Broton.

"Very good, Commander. We are descending—now!"

The Zygon ship dropped out of the clouds and landed in a deserted quarry. It hid beneath the overhang of the carved-out cliff face like a crab under a rock. Broton surveyed the scene on his monitor screens. Not perfect, but it would have to do. He knew his crippled ship

111

would never fly again. He had staked everyting on this last desperate gamble for power.

In his cell, the Doctor heard an amplified Zygon voice echoing through the ship. "Prepare to receive a message from Commander Broton!"

The Doctor made a loud and vulgar raspberry.

Then came Broton's familiar tones. "From this moment, all outward signals are forbidden. All available power is necessary to maintain the screening signal. Internal operations will be maintained on half-power."

"Paranoid half-wit!" snorted the Doctor. Then he looked up. The voices had come from a bell-shaped device on the wall. Like the Zygon ship itself, it appeared half manufactured and half grown. More to pass the time than for any definite reason, the Doctor started to dismantle it with his sonic screwdriver. He'd already tried the door, but it was too tough. Meanwhile, even this little bit of sabotage was better than nothing.

The Brigadier stared at Benton in sheer disbelief. "*All* of them?"

"I'm afraid so, sir. There's a complete radar blackout all over the country."

"I see. Well, we'll just have to hope for visual contact when they come down—if they ever do. Carry on, Mr. Benton."

Benton saluted and went to supervise UNIT's

112

departure arrangements. In the doorway, he passed Harry and Sarah. The Brigadier looked up. "Just in time you two. Find anything?"

Sarah shook her head. "No. Not a thing. Any news of the spacecraft?"

"Last report had it traveling south over Leicester. Then we lost it. Those creatures have managed to cause a complete radar blackout. There's something else though—reports from shipping on the East Coast. We've had several accounts of a large underwater object traveling south at high speed."

Sarah's eyes widened. "And we can all guess what that is—can't we?"

Broton looked at the tiny dot moving slowly across the tracking screen. "How far is the Skarasen from target now?"

"One hundred and fifty-two Earth miles, Commander. It is approaching the mouth of the estuary."

"That is close enough. Sever contact. The activator will bring it to the target from that range."

Obediently the Zygon pressed the control nodule, and the screen went dark. Broton stood brooding for a moment. Everything was going well. His plans were almost complete. Soon this entire planet would be his—yet something was missing. He needed to tell someone of his cleverness, to overawe someone with the might of

Zygon technology. There was only one suitable candidate—the Doctor. Broton decided to make one last attempt to bring his prisoner to a properly respectful frame of mind.

The Doctor was happily completing the dismantling of the loudspeaker when he heard Broton approaching his cell. Hastily he shoved the speaker back into position. He was seated cross-legged on the floor in a pose of complete relaxation when Broton entered. He noted the presence of two Zygon guards outside the cell, and reluctantly abandoned thoughts of escape, at least for the moment.

He looked up at Broton and smiled politely. "Is this a social call?"

Broton hissed angrily. Once more the discussion was beginning wrongly. Something about this primitive being always seemed to shake his composure. "Do you admire Zygon technology, human?" he demanded peevishly.

The Doctor yawned. "I'm *not* human, and as for technology—well, I've seen better."

Broton ignored the first part of this remark. Since these primitives had not yet achieved true space flight, *everyone* on the planet must be human, except of course for the all-conquering Zygons. He concentrated on the Doctor's slur on Zygon achievements. "Better than this—human?"

The Doctor saw Broton's form shimmer and blur. Seconds later the Duke of Forgill stood

114

before him, this time dressed not in shooting tweeds, but in immaculate morning dress.

The Doctor clapped politely. "Very impressive," he said admiringly. "Yes, very good indeed."

Broton looked at him suspiciously. At last the prisoner was expressing proper sentiments—though still with an air of mockery.

"Tell me," asked the Doctor casually, "why do you keep the originals alive?"

"It is necessary to re-register a body print at frequent intervals. Otherwise the original pattern dies."

"I hope you're not planning to duplicate me?"

"There is no need for more concealment. You seem the most intelligent of the primitives on this planet. You can serve us, or die!"

Ignoring this offer, the Doctor said, "But you do still need a replica of the Duke?"

"We have *one* further use for that shape—and one only."

"A formal occasion, I take it?"

Broton smiled mockingly. "Perhaps."

The Doctor saw Broton wasn't going to tell him anything specific. "I gather we've landed. Where are we?"

"You ask many questions."

"Well, it's the only way to learn anything," said the Doctor reasonably. "Here's another for you. When does the great operation begin— your conquest of this planet?"

As the Doctor had guessed, Broton was unable to resist the opportunity for more boasting. "Phase One is already complete."

"And what do you intend to do with the planet when you have it?" the Doctor enquired politely. "I mean it's rather a big place for just you and your ship's crew."

"There are many other Zygon ships roaming the galaxy, since our planet was destroyed in a solar catastrophe. Once this planet is ours, I shall summon them here to their new home."

"Do you think they'll like it here? Earth is surely very different from your home world."

"That can be remedied. The other ships will arrive gradually over several centuries. We Zygons are a long-lived race. While we are waiting for them, I shall restructure this planet."

The Doctor gave a whistle of genuine admiration. "I'll say this for you, Broton, you certainly think big. How do you propose to achieve that?"

Broton made a lordly gesture. "The polar ice caps must go, the mean temperature will be raised several degrees, thousands of lakes constructed with the right mineral elements to breed more herds of Skarasen. I shall re-create my own world here on Earth."

"Using the human population as forced labor, I take it?"

Broton nodded. "Human labor and Zygon

116

technology. The task is challenging, but not impossible."

The Doctor shook his head. "You underestimate the human race, Broton. They'll never consent to be slaves of the Zygons."

"They will, Doctor—once I have demonstrated my power."

Still in the immaculate form of the Duke of Forgill, Broton turned and strode from the cell, closing the door behind him.

The Doctor took the partially dismantled speaker from the wall and stared thoughtfully at it. The first glimmerings of a plan began to form in his mind. It was a good plan, with only one flaw. The slightest error in calculations would result in his death.

11

Escape!

In the usually busy Communications Room at UNIT's London HQ, Sarah and Benton sat looking gloomily at a pile of silent equipment. The Doctor's tracing equipment had been brought down and installed, but it registered nothing. Benton unwrapped some chocolate and passed a piece to Sarah. They sat munching sadly.

"Something's *bound* to happen soon, miss," Benton tried to be consoling. "I mean, if these creatures *have* got a plan, they'll have to make a move."

"It's the Doctor I'm worried about. For all we know he could be dead."

"Come on, now. Take more than that lot to kill the Doctor. He's probably planning his escape right now."

Sarah managed a smile. "I know. It's just not hearing anything."

Benton hurriedly swallowed his last piece of chocolate as the Brigadier bustled into the room. "Any news, sir?" he asked a little indistinctly.

"Nothing on the spaceship. But the undersea object has been sighted again. The Navy's sending some frigates."

Everyone looked up eagerly as the telephone rang. Benton took the call. His eyes widened and he gave a silent whistle. "Yes, he's here. I'll put you through now, sir." Benton covered the mouthpiece and hissed. "It's for you, sir. The Prime Minister, from Stanbridge House."

The Brigadier raised his eyes in a silent prayer and took the receiver. "Yes, sir . . . absolutely, sir, no public announcement. Discreet action . . . discreet but *resolute* action. Yes, sir, I'll keep you informed." Very gently he replaced the receiver—Sarah guessed he was resisting the temptation to crash it down. She could imagine the sort of instructions he'd been given. He was to take firm action, without of course being rash. Whatever happened, it was the Brigadier's head on the block.

"Politicians!" exploded the Brigadier. "All very well for them."

Sarah gave him a sympathetic smile. "What *are* you going to do, Brigadier?"

"Just what I always do, Miss Smith. I shall act as I think best."

The Doctor had succeeded in disentangling the twisted mass of roots and ganglia behind the Zygon loudspeaker. He regarded the maze of glowing and humming power lines. Organic crystallography wasn't really his forte, but he thought he'd worked it all out. The glowing crystal *here* was a part of the main power system. This smaller cable was connected to the ship's transmission equipment. Somehow the two had to be linked—and there was only one way.

The Doctor braced himself, and ripped the vine-like cable free of the socket. He gripped the "live" end firmly. By stretching his other arm he could—just—reach the power crystal. "Now for the big question," he said softly. "Is half power lethal?" There was only one way to find out. The Doctor lunged and grasped the power crystal with his free hand, bridging the two sections of the ship's power network with his body. Immediately an immense burst of dynacronic power flowed *through* the Doctor's body and into the transmission system. He twisted and writhed in agony. Sweat poured from him, but grimly he held on. A loud, burbling shriek filled the entire ship.

As the Doctor had hoped, his action had two effects. It cut out the Zygon screening network, which had caused the radar blackout and was now concealing the position of the ship. More important, it betrayed that position with a powerful diastellic signal, as easy to pick up as a smoke signal in the empty desert. If only the Brigadier was using the tracing equipment properly, thought the Doctor. Then consciousness started to fade away. Despite his fierce determination, his fingers began slipping from the power crystal.

In the control room Broton, now back in his Zygon form, turned to his chief engineer in consternation. "A relay has jammed on the diastellic circuit!"

The Zygon checked his controls. "No, Commander. The circuit panel is in order."

"Trace the source immediately. We must stop the transmission."

The engineer bent over a screen which showed the ship's power network.

"It is registering on the internal power feed. From the prison area."

"The Doctor!" said Broton grimly. They set off for the cell at a run.

At UNIT HQ, Benton leaned eagerly over his equipment. "I'm getting something, sir—look!" On the Doctor's trace screen, the Zygon signal was registering like a fiery beacon.

The Brigadier rubbed his hands. "Now if the Tower squad are on their toes—we've got 'em."

A special UNIT squad had installed a set of the Doctor's tracing equipment on top of the Post Office Tower. Two traces were needed to give an accurate fix. The phone rang almost immediately. Benton grabbed it. "Yes, we got it too, clear as day. Right, give me the bearing."

Benton jotted down some figures on the pad that already held his readings—and ran to the map table. He made quick calculations, then used a big plastic ruler to draw two lines across the map. Triumphantly he pointed to the spot where they intersected. "Here, sir. Just beyond Brentford." He looked closer at the big ordnance survey map. "Seems to be some kind of quarry, sir. Anyway—we know where they are!"

By the time Broton reached the cell, the signal had already died away. The Doctor lay motionless on the floor.

The Zygon engineer examined him. "He is dead."

"Naturally. The dynacronic power destroyed him. No human being could withstand it." Broton regarded the Doctor with something close to admiration. "I underestimated his intelligence. But he underestimated the power of organic crystallography."

"Do you think they will succeed in tracing us?"

"It is unlikely. The signal was brief and their human equipment is primitive. Nevertheless, I shall bring the plan forward. Come!"

The Zygons strode from the cell, giving no further thought to the body of the Doctor, not even bothering to close the cell door. Once they were gone, the Doctor opened his eyes. The trouble with Broton was that he simply didn't *listen*. After all, thought the Doctor, I did tell him I wasn't human.

Weak and shaky after his ordeal, but still very much alive, the Doctor struggled to his feet.

In the control room Broton went over the final details of his plan. "Distance?" he snapped.

"The Skarasen is fifty Earth miles from target, Commander."

"Excellent. It is time for me to place the activator. Humanity is at our feet!" Once more Broton began to shimmer and blur, as he changed his shape to that of the Duke of Forgill.

After a bit of deep breathing and a few of his special setting-up exercises, the Doctor felt not quite as good as new, but almost. He crept cautiously from his cell and found himself in the area where the imprisoned humans stood motionless in their cubicles. The Doctor studied the circuitry around them for a moment, then began operating controls.

There was a low humming and after a moment the Duke of Forgill, the *real* Duke of Forgill, opened his eyes and asked the classic question, "Where am I?"

"In a spaceship," the Doctor replied briskly. "Please don't ask any more questions, your Grace, there's no time to explain." Hastily the Doctor started reviving the other prisoners.

Broton gave final instructions to his chief engineer. "In two minutes shut down all diastellic transmission, and maintain monitor contact."

"Understood, Commander."

Broton paused, savoring the moment. Final

victory was so near now. "When Phase Two is completed," he said grandly, "I shall broadcast my demands to the world!"

At a nod from Broton, the engineer touched the nodule that opened the special exit. A panel opened in the side of the Zygon ship, and Broton, Warlord of the Zygons, wearing for the last time the shape of the Duke of Forgill, stepped out to conquer the world.

Inside the ship the Doctor, watched by a confused group of newly released prisoners, was pointing his sonic screwdriver at a mushroom-like projection in the ceiling.

"What are you up to now, man?" grumbled the Duke, inclined to be testy after his long imprisonment.

"This is a fire sensor, your Grace—and if I apply sufficient concentrated heat . . ."

A clangorous alarm rang through the ship. The Doctor grinned. "All of you, back into your alcoves and feign death. We'll see how good their fire drill is, eh?"

Panic-stricken Zygons soon began to rush along the corridor, hunting for the source of the fire. All Zygon ships are highly inflammable, and the fear of fire built deep into the Zygon consciousness caused them to react with hysterical fear. As soon as the Zygons were past, the Doctor emerged from hiding, and led his little group to the now-empty control room. As the automatic door closed behind them, the Doctor tapped the Caber on the shoulder and pointed out a projecting root, rather like a gear-stick.

"You see that? It controls the vacuum mechanism that opens the door. Just break it off, will you?"

The gnarled lever was astonishingly tough, but the Caber was astonishingly strong. Muscles bulging, he ripped it clear from its socket. When the Zygon crew realized they'd been

The Doctor looked around the control room the door remained obstinately closed against them. They began to scrabble at it with their claw-like hands, hissing in rage and terror.

The Doctor looked round the control room thoughtfully, and pointed to a complex mechanism set a little apart from the other controls. "Anyone know what this is?"

The baffled group shook their heads. "You tell us," said Sister Lamont in her soft Highland voice.

"It's a Self-Destructor Unit," said the Doctor rather sadly. "And it works like—this!" He tugged on the control nodule, and the Destructor Unit began to hum with power.

The group of released prisoners looked at it in silent wonder. The Doctor touched another nodule and a hatch opened in the side of the ship. In a conversational tone the Doctor added, "We've got about sixty seconds before the whole ship blows up!"

This was something the captives *could* understand, and if the Doctor hadn't stood aside he would have been trampled in the rush.

In the quarry, the Brigadier checked that the hastily set-up cordon of soldiers around the spaceship was properly in place. Beside him stood Harry Sullivan, loaded down with the latest thing in thermic lances, ready to cut his way into the Zygon ship. Sarah, who'd been allowed to come only on the strict understanding that she stayed in the landrover, looked on anxiously, waiting for the attack to start.

Taking a deep breath, the Brigadier prepared to give the order to attack. Before he could get the words out, a hatch in the ship's side opened and a motley assortment of people rushed out, the Doctor close behind them. At the sight of the Brigadier and his men the Doctor yelled, "Get back, all of you. Back and down!"

The Brigadier relayed the order. "All right, everybody. Pull back and take cover!"

The circle of men around the spaceship suddenly expanded as everyone started to run *away* from it. Sarah ran up a slight rise and turned to call the Doctor.

"Doctor, over here!"

The Doctor came sprinting up to her. "Get *down*," he yelled, and Sarah threw herself to the ground. There came a rumbling explosion, a blinding white flash, and then silence.

Cautiously Sarah raised her head and looked back at the spaceship. She saw—nothing! The Self-Destructor Unit, as efficient as all Zygon technology, had left nothing of the spaceship and its crew but fine white ash, which drifted away on the wind.

The Doctor stood up, helped Sarah to her feet, and gave her a quick hug of greeting. Before she could say anything Harry and the Brigadier came running up. Harry pounded the Doctor on the back. "Well done, Doctor, well done!"

The Doctor winced, dodged the next exuberant thump, and turned to the Brigadier. "Well, Brigadier, was that a big enough noise for you?" His face was sad. He'd hated destroying the ship and its crew, but it had been the only way to prevent the loss of still more human lives.

The Brigadier gave a contented nod. "Congratulations, Doctor. Our troubles are over."

"Don't be too sure, old chap."

"Why?" broke in Harry. "The Zygons *are* finished now, aren't they?"

"Well, not exactly. I'm afraid Broton got away."

The Brigadier wasn't worried. "Soon round *him* up. Broton by himself isn't much of a threat." He glanced at the Doctor's face. "Or is he?"

"Don't forget, there's still the monster, Brigadier. Broton controls it."

"It's been spotted swimming along the coast," said Harry. "Seems to be heading this way—and we still don't know what he intends to do with it."

The Doctor frowned. "It's almost certain to be some piece of spectacular destruction somewhere in London. And there's an obvious way for the monster to approach . . ."

"The river," snapped the Brigadier. "It was last seen near the estuary."

"Exactly. With one of the highest tides of the year running, it could come right into London."

Harry tried to think of likely targets. "The docks? The bridges?"

"I don't think so, Harry. Broton's looking for something *really* spectacular."

"Just before I picked up your signal," said the Brigadier slowly. "I had a panic call from the P.M. He was speaking from Stanbridge House. *That's* on the river . . ."

"What's happening there?"

"The Fourth International Energy Conference. It opens today. The place will be full of VIPs from all over the world."

"A good place for Broton to make his power felt internationally. That could be it, Brigadier."

"Very tight security, though. He'd need a top-level pass to get in."

"But he'll *have* a pass," Sarah burst out. "He'll be looking like the Duke of Forgill, remember—and the Duke is President of the Scottish Energy Commission. That must be why Broton took the Duke's document case—he's going to attend the Conference!"

Monster in the Thames

Deep beneath the swollen flood tide of the River Thames, a giant shape was moving steadily up river. It couldn't hope to evade detection any longer. But that wasn't important. Soon the Skarasen would be at its target. And there was no power on Earth strong enough to stop it carrying out its mission.

In UNIT's Communications Room, Benton and his team had monitored the monster's progress. All they could do was watch. The Doctor had warned that nothing less than an atomic bomb would have the slightest effect on the Skarasen. It was impossible to use a weapon of sufficient power without destroying all London as well. Any lesser weapon might well have the effect of angering the monster, perhaps sending it on a killing rampage through the city.

In Stanbridge House, an imposing new conference hall on the edge of the Thames, a packed mob of VIPs milled and jostled, enjoying their free champagne at the reception which was following the formal opening of the conference. Security guards were everywhere, discreetly checking passes and surveying the crowd for intruders, and there were policemen at all the doors.

His Grace the Duke of Forgill moved quietly through the guests, a well-known and respected figure. He seemed rather weary and abstracted, nodding in reply to the greetings of old friends, but never stopping to talk.

He crossed the main hall and left by one of the side entrances, showing his pass to the policeman on guard, who touched his helmet respectfully. "Need a breath of air," explained the Duke. "Terrible crush in there."

Once out of the policeman's sight the Duke moved not upward toward the open terrace that overlooked the river, but downstairs to the basement. He slipped through an unmarked service door and followed a concrete staircase leading to the cellars. At the end of a bare stone corridor he came to a metal door marked NO ADMITTANCE, pushed it open and went inside. Another flight of steps led down into darkness.

In the conference hall, scandal and confusion was breaking out among the delegates. There seemed to be some kind of a flap on. As if it weren't enough to have policemen and plain-clothes security guards everywhere, there were soldiers turning up, armed men with UNIT flashes on their shoulders. They were led by a full-blown Brigadier, an odd-looking chap wearing a floppy hat and a long scarf, a young man and a very pretty girl. The delegates muttered and grumbled over their Government champagne, wondering what was going on.

The Doctor, the Brigadier, Harry and Sarah squeezed their way out of the main hall and assembled in a quiet corridor. "No sign of him in there," said the Brigadier. "Still, we know he's here somewhere—Security checked him into the building."

"What's in this building—besides the hall itself?" asked the Doctor.

The Brigadier produced a plan. "Catering section, river terrace. Usual service area in the basement."

"Right, Brigadier, you take a party and search around here. I'll take a look in the basement."

Road and river traffic along the Thames embankment were thrown into utter confusion when a monstrous head on the end of a long sinuous neck broke the surface of the water. Ignoring the panic-stricken screams of passers-by the monster weaved its head to and fro for a moment, as if taking a bearing, then plunged once again into the river, swimming steadily toward Stanbridge House. . . .

Sarah kept close to the Doctor as they moved through the gloomy basement corridors. She'd followed him automatically, but now she was wondering why she hadn't chosen to stay upstairs with the Brigadier and Harry.

At the end of a bare stone corridor, they came to a plain metal door bearing a NO AD-

MITTANCE sign. "Probably the cellars," said the Doctor. "Let's take a look."

He opened the door and saw stairs leading down into darkness. The Doctor found a light switch by the door and flicked it, but nothing happened. "That's funny," he said. "The light's not working."

Sarah giggled nervously. "Someone should tell the Energy Congress."

The Doctor flung the door open wide, so that light from the corridor streamed onto the steps. "Stay here," he ordered, and went down into the darkness. Sarah peered after him.

A familiar hissing voice spoke from the darkness below. "I thought you were dead, Doctor."

"Loose thinking, Broton," the Doctor said lightly, peering into the gloom to detect his enemy.

"This time I shall make certain," said the voice coldly.

The Doctor spoke over his shoulder. "Sarah, get the Brigadier."

Turning back to face the darkness, he said, "Broton, your spaceship has been destroyed, and this building is surrounded by troops. You are alone on this planet. You *must* surrender."

Broton appeared from the darkness, climbing the stairs until he was visible in the light. He had reverted to his own Zygon form, and he held a Zygon device in his hand about the size and shape of an old-fashioned pocket watch.

"This is the Activator! With it I control the

Skarasen. I can destroy your planet, or be its master. That is the choice I offer your world."

Sarah, frozen in terror, was still at the Doctor's shoulder. Suddenly Broton ran up the steps, dodged past the Doctor and lunged for her at amazing speed, stinging claw outstretched. The Doctor grappled with him and yelled, "Run, Sarah!"

She tore back down the corridor calling, "Brigadier! Where are you, Brigadier? This way!"

Luckily the Brigadier had finished his search of the catering area and was on his way to find the Doctor. Sarah turned a corner and ran straight into him. "This way—the Doctor's found him." Sarah led them back to the cellar at a run.

The Doctor and Broton rolled down the steps and wrestled desperately in the cellar darkness. The Doctor was gripping Broton by the wrists, concentrating on keeping the stinging claws away from him. With a sudden convulsive heave Broton broke free and sent the Doctor hurtling across a pile of crates. The Doctor lay there winded for a moment, and Broton crouched over him.

The Brigadier and his men appeared in the doorway, shining torches into the darkness. The first soldier through the door ran down to grapple with Broton, who jabbed with his stinging claws, and killed the man with a savage blast of power. As the soldier dropped, the Brigadier shouted, "Doctor, keep down!" and emptied his service revolver into Broton's body.

As the crash of shots died away, Broton stood swaying a moment, green eyes ablaze with hatred. "The Skarasen will destroy you all," he hissed, and crumpled to the floor.

The Doctor got to his feet and examined Broton's hands. Both were empty. He stared wildly around the cellar. "The signal device. We must find it, quickly. Either it got dropped in the fight, or Broton's hidden it. Brigadier, you'll have to evacuate the building. The Skarasen will tear down this building to get at that device."

With the aid of the torches, it took only minutes to search the small bare room. The device was nowhere to be seen. The Doctor stood in the middle of the room, his mind racing, "Broton had the device just before we struggled. Now where would he have wanted . . ." A delighted grin broke over the Doctor's face. He slipped his hand into his own coat pocket, and when he brought it out, there lay the device. "A trier to the last, our friend Broton. He obviously hoped the monster would crunch *me* up to get this."

A sudden shattering roar came from the direction of the river. It was clearly audible, even in the cellar. "The Skarasen," said the Doctor. "Come on, we've got to get to the terrace." He ran up the stairs, the others close behind him.

The river terrace high above the Thames was one of the special features of Stanbridge House.

But none of the architects had envisaged the view which met the eyes of the Doctor and his friends as they ran up to the terrace parapet. They found themselves literally face to face with the monster, since the creature's long neck brought its head well up to the level of the terrace. They stared for a moment at the great rolling eyes, and the rows of savage teeth.

"It's huge," gasped Sarah.

"Oh, I've seen bigger," said the Doctor disparagingly. He held up the Zygon device between finger and thumb. "Here, boy, here!"

There was another roar as the great head lunged toward them.

Quite undismayed the Doctor shouted, "Here boy! Fetch it!"

As if throwing a ball for a dog, the Doctor aimed the device in an arc, just above the creature's head. The monster's neck swung around and the teeth clashed down on the signaling device, snapping it up like a biscuit. With a tremendous splash, the monster sank back beneath the water. For a moment they could see the great dark shape swimming down river, then it disappeared into the depths. "On its way home, no doubt," said the Doctor.

Harry looked at him. "Home? Where?"

"Loch Ness, Harry—after all, that's the only home it knows."

As they turned to leave the terrace, Sarah couldn't help wishing the Skarasen a safe journey. It wasn't evil in itself—it had only obeyed the commands of its Zygon masters. Soon the old stories would be true at last. There really would be a monster in Loch Ness.

The Brigadier climbed slowly up the Scottish hillside, deep in conversation with the Duke of Forgill. Ahead, he could see the Doctor, Harry, and Sarah climbing the steep track toward the TARDIS.

"The Cabinet have accepted my report, your Grace," he was saying, "but the whole affair is now an official secret."

"You mean it never happened?"

"Exactly, your Grace."

The Duke grunted. He was far from certain what had been happening since he and his retainers were kidnapped by the Zygons, but it was clear that the Brigadier's odd-looking friend had got him out of a very nasty spot, and he was grateful for that. He'd insisted on meeting them at the station, and driving them up the hill to recover the TARDIS.

As they approached the others, the Duke said, "Funny thing, y'know, but as I was driving to the station to meet you people I could swear I caught a glimpse of something big submerging in the loch."

"But you're not sure?" asked Sarah.

The Duke shook his head. "Sun was in my eyes. This what you've come to collect?" He pointed to the blue police call box, still perched on the hillside.

"That's right, your Grace," said the Doctor proudly. "This is the TARDIS."

"How you going to get it down the hill? Get some of my people to help you if you like. The Caber could do it single-handed."

"Very kind, your Grace, but that won't be necessary. I think I'll drive it back to London. I can be there five minutes ago."

Sarah gave him a sceptical look. "Are you sure about that, Doctor?"

The Doctor was always indignant at any reflection upon his ability to control the TARDIS. "Of course I am. I shall simply slip into the Time Vortex, then reset the co-ordinates." He produced the TARDIS key and opened the door. "Who's coming with me?" He looked hopefully around the group.

"No thank you, Doctor. Never again!" said the Brigadier firmly. He had very disturbing memories of his one trip in the TARDIS.

"How about you, Harry?"

Harry took an instinctive step back. Getting into the TARDIS had involved him in a series of adventures he preferred not to think about. Now he was on Earth again, he intended to stay there. "I'll stick to Inter-City this time, thanks all the same, Doctor."

"Sarah?"

Sarah thought longingly of the comfort and safety of a first class compartment on the London train. Then she saw the disappointment on the Doctor's face. "All right, Doctor," she said reluctantly. "But only if we go straight back to London."

The Doctor looked hurt. "I promise you, Sarah. Straight back."

Sarah took a deep breath, said goodbye to the others, and stepped into the TARDIS. The Doctor waved a cheerful farewell and followed her in, closing the door behind them. Harry and the Brigadier exchanged looks of resignation. The Duke glanced from one to the other, wondering what the blazes was going on.

A curious groaning, wheezing noise filled the air, and the blue police box faded away. The Duke was far too well-bred to show any surprise. Besides, when a chap's been held prisoner in a spaceship and impersonated by an alien monster, it's not so easy to surprise him. He looked at the Brigadier and said impassively, "Did they have return tickets?"

"Yes—I think so, your Grace—why?"

"You should have taken them and got a refund, man. Thought you were supposed to be a Scotsman!"

The Brigadier chuckled politely at the aristocratic joke, and all three started walking down to the Duke's station wagon. The Brigadier wondered where the Doctor and Sarah would end up. He was pretty convinced of one thing. For all the Doctor's protestations—it *wasn't* likely to be anywhere as ordinary as London!

"What we always knew about Sherlock
Holmes when he supposedly fell to his
death at the Reichenbach Falls, we now
know about Solar Pons—he is not dead;
he has just been hiding."

—*St. Louis Post-Dispatch*

THE ADVENTURES OF

by
Basil Copper
based on the characters
and series created by
August Derleth

*Come, once again, to Number 7B Praed Street, where Solar
Pons, the master of deduction, awaits your arrival. Slouched
in the cozy cavern of his armchair, his keen eyes fixed on
the door, Solar Pons puffs thoughtfully on his pipe, ponder-
ing the strange and soul-chilling cases he has selected for
your mystification.*

Over forty years ago, when August Derleth inherited the

mantle of Sir Arthur Conan Doyle, he created in Solar Pons a detective whose genius cannot be matched—perhaps not even by Sherlock Holmes himself! Now the pen has passed into the hand of the noted British author, Basil Copper, whose superlative storytelling abilities will astound and delight faithful followers and mystery lovers alike.

Here is the brilliant Solar Pons at his very best . . . clutching at elusive clues as he briskly sets apace into the ominous alleyways of old London in chase of crime. If you've not yet joined us in the eternal hunt, you are about to discover a new joy in a tradition that, alas, may have been lost forever, were it not for the reappearance of the remarkably ingenious and incomparable Solar Pons, whose entrancing effect on dyed-in-the wool aficionados of detection is, indeed, elementary. It is time now to begin. The game's afoot!

(*The following pages have been excerpted from* The Dossier of Solar Pons, *#8 in the series, in which Dr. Lyndon Parker, Pons's faithful companion, relates "The Adventure of the Ipi Idol".*)

More than an hour had passed and the lights had long been extinguished. I eased my position in the chair and waved my hand to dispel the heavy waves of blue smoke from Pons's pipe.

"Patience, Parker," he said softly. "I fancy the time is at hand. If he is to strike it must be done soon because he knows we are on the ground."

We had only a bedside lamp burning in the room and all the time we had been here Pons had been alert, listening for every footfall in the corridor. Half a dozen times he had darted to the room door, opening it a crack, surveying the corridor outside and then returning to his seat. There were two wall sconces still burning in the passage outside, leaving long stretches of shadow, and I understood from Pons that it was Colonel d'Arcy's habit to leave lights on all night whenever he had house guests.

Twice had the surly figure of Vickers been seen by Pons passing along the corridor during that time, but Pons had only smiled at my fulminations and had bidden me to be patient. Now there had been a deep silence for some while though my companion assured me that lights still shone beneath some doors, including that of Colonel d'Arcy.

I had risen from my chair and was taking a turn about the room when Pons jumped swiftly to his feet, holding his finger to his lips. At almost the same instant a terrible scream reechoed throughout the house. It was a woman's voice, hoarse and resonant with terror and it seemed to come from next door. Pons had already flung open the door, revolver in hand.

"As quickly as you can, Parker. It is life and death!"

I was swiftly at his heels, revolver drawn, as Pons flung himself at the door of Colonel d'Arcy's room. He hurled it open without ceremony. I shall never forget the sight that greeted us. The room was lit only by one solitary bedside lamp which threw a subdued glow across the apartment.

The bed coverlets had been thrown back but our attention was riveted on the end of the bed where the figure of a beautiful girl crouched, a look of absolute terror on her chalk-white face. The body of Miss Claire Mortimer was rigid with shock and horror. She was clad only in a dressing gown and her dark hair was awry and falling across her face.

"There, Parker, there!" said Solar Pons, his iron grip at my wrist.

I wrenched my glance from the frozen figure of the girl up toward the pillow. At first I could see nothing, then, from the tumbled white sheets, flickered the greenish coils of a snake. Its tongue darted from its mouth and a sibilant hissing noise filled the chamber. My throat was dry and my hand unsteady, but Pon's voice brought me to myself.

"A green mamba, Parker. The most deadly snake in all Africa! Your shot, I think."

I raised my revolver, hardly conscious of what I was doing. Yet I was myself again, my nerves calmed by Pons's reassuring presence. He moved closer to the girl, inch by inch, his derringer at the ready.

The crack of my pistol, the acrid sting of powder and the flash were followed by a rain of feathers from the bed, and the bullet cut a vicious gouge in the planking of the floor beyond. Splinters flew in the air as the snake writhed for an instant and then was still.

"Well done, Parker!" said Pons, supporting the fainting

143

girl and dragging her from the bed. I ran to his side and helped him move here to a chair.

"See to that thing, Parker. Make sure it is dead."

Perspiration was running down my cheeks, but my nerves were steady now as I cautiously approached the bed.

"My aim was true, Pons," I said, unable to keep the pride from my voice. Footsteps were sounding in the corridor now, and the room seemed full of people. I was only vaguely aware of Bradshaw, Tolliver, Mrs. Mortimer, and the dark visage of Vickers.

Light flooded the room from a ceiling fixture, and at the same instant I managed to cover the remains of the snake with the bedding. Pons shot me a glance of approval. The bearded face of Colonel d'Arcy appeared. He elbowed his way through without ceremony.

"Good God, Mr. Pons! Claire! What on earth has happened?"

"The lady has had a nightmare," said Pons gently. "All is well now. But I think it would be best if she spent the remainder of the night with her mother. And I should keep this room locked if I were you."

The colonel instantly grasped the situation.

"It is nothing, ladies and gentlemen. Would you please return to your rooms. I very much regret the disturbance."

The sobbing girl, soothed by her mother, was led from the room, and the remaining guests, with curious glances, shortly followed. Our host hurried away, leaving Pons and me alone in that suddenly sinister room.

"I don't understand, Pons," I said.

Solar Pons ran a finger along his jaw, which was grimly set.

"I am not entirely clear myself, Parker," he said. "But we shall no doubt learn more in a moment."

Indeed, our host returned almost at once and faced us somberly, locking the door behind him.

"I cannot thank you enough, gentlemen. If anything had happened to Claire . . . What was it?"

I pulled back the bedding. Colonel d'Arcy surveyed the mamba with sick loathing on his face. He clenched his fists and his features began to suffuse with blood.

"By God, Mr. Pons, we must discover the wicked mind behind this . . ."

"It is almost over, Colonel," said Pons quietly. "Though I do not know how Miss Mortimer came to be here."

"She complained of a draft in her room," said our host. "Mine was the more comfortable so I gave it to her. The fireplace has more heat, for one thing."

Pons nodded.

"Evidently, he could not have known that," he murmured. "I am afraid Parker and I have made a mess of your floor . . ."

Colonel d'Arcy stared at us in amazement. He came forward and wrung my hand, then turned to Pons.

"I am not an emotional man, gentlemen, but Miss Mortimer means more to me than anything in the world."

"I understand that, Colonel," said Pons, frowning down at the thing that still lay in bloody tatters on the bed. "But it will not stop here. Our man knows we are on him. The shot alone would have warned him. He will act quickly. We must act more quickly still."

Colonel d'Arcy looked bewildered.

"I am in your hands, Mr. Pons. What do you want me to do?"

"I think this evil man will strike again before the night is out. This time at you, Colonel. I want you to go to my room or Parker's and spend the night there. No one but the three of us must know of this."

"Anything you say, Mr. Pons. What do you intend to do?"

Pons went to stand by the fireplace, holding out his thin hands to the glowing embers. His lean, feral face had seldom looked more grim.

"First, I would like the disposition of the guests this evening and the exact location of their rooms."

"That is easily done," said the colonel.

Pons listened attentively as he gave us the information. He nodded with satisfaction.

"Ironic is it not, Parker?"

"I do not understand, Pons."

"No matter. You will in due time."

He turned briskly to the colonel.

145

"We must spend the rest of the night in your room, Colonel. I fancy a revolver or a stick will be adequate protection against the menace of the Ipi idol."

He looked at me, his eyes alight with excitement.

"Come, Parker. The game's afoot!"